THE

GOBLIN

Steven Marks

THE GOBLIN

The Goblin is a work of fiction. Though some of the
cities and towns actually exist they are used in a
fictitious manner for purposes of this work. All
characters are works of fiction and any names or
characteristics similar to any person past, present or
future are coincidental.

DEDICATION

For Jesse, who is the Caretaker.

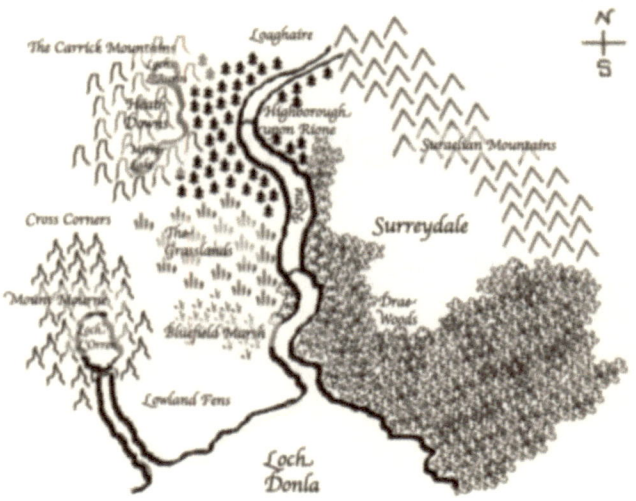

CHAPTER 1

*T*hroughout time, the race of creatures known as goblins has invariably been portrayed as evil, sometimes clever, often mindless, and easily led by those in power, but to the victor go the spoils, and also the ability to write history. This is the story of Thrax, a goblin who fell from the path and discovered that truth, even if universally accepted, is not always based on fact. Though my role in this drama was not significant, I was a witness to many of the events and can vouch for the accuracy of this account. My name is Jesse, and I have been the Caretaker of the Gardens of Surreydale and the entire surrounding county for many a year.

Our story begins on a still evening in late September. The farmers of Surreydale had just completed their day's work as the sun slipped below the edge of the world, framed by a halo of orange and gold. The pale harvest moon was rising and the quiet of the evening cast a spell of contentment over the town. It was one of those soft, magical fall days, and no one was in a hurry for it to end. Neighbors gathered around steel drums, burning the chaff in warm fires, and speaking softly, telling tales passed down by their grandparents and great-grandparents of heroes and warriors and battles of long ago.

It was an unlikely night for a goblin attack, though raiders had been in the area for weeks. A few cattle had gone missing and one of the townsfolk had lost a horse. But goblins, as you know, are great, noisy creatures, not at all adept at stealth, and so generally only appear openly when the night is dark and the wind is high.

This particular pack was made up of very young goblins, the oldest having probably seen no more than fifteen summers, which may explain the unfortunate timing. The element of surprise, in the fact that it was so bold a venture, was certainly in their favor. What they lacked in experience they might have made up for in size and ferocity. Unfortunately the goblins failed to consider that the farmers had weapons immediately at hand, tools of the harvest: scythes, sickles, axes, and knives.

The battle was savage, and short. The goblins bore the worst of it. A few of the townsfolk had minor scrapes, but at least three of the goblins were killed and several were mortally wounded. Thrax was one of the wounded and, though he tried his best to flee with the rest, he soon found himself falling face down in a field to the south of town.

Now as a rule, goblins don't have friends as you or I might have. They don't even have family to speak of. They live as nomads on the land, stealing and killing for food. Goblins travel in packs because it is more efficient, not because they care for each other's company. When times are hard and food is scarce, they are quite as likely to prey upon one another as upon anyone or anything else. There was, therefore, no one to help Thrax when he fell, at least not one of the other goblins.

As he lay there, dying, I think it unlikely that he was pondering the ethereal nature of life, as an elf or a man might have done. He was more likely raging against the elves that had struck him down. Thrax was at that time only ten years old and this was his first experience of battle, however abbreviated. He had yet to kill anything other than wild game or cattle. I'm quite sure he never thought then that he would live to become one of the most infamous and feared goblins of his time.

CHAPTER 2

*I*t happened that the field in which Thrax had fallen belonged to a very good and influential elf named Amias Strong, one of only two physicians in Surreydale. He and his wife Clare, father-in-law Tomas, daughter Kira, and son Finn had heard the shouts and rushed outside, but the battle was far enough away and was of such a brief duration that none of them had time to join the fray. Thrax was totally unaware that five pairs of eyes, six if you count mine, had followed his flight across the north end of the field, and that there was a great disparity in the feelings inspired in the close-knit family by his head-long fall into the dirt.

"Amias and I will take care of it," Tomas said, setting his mouth in a firm line and tightening his grip on his sword. "Best to take the children inside."

"Unlikely, Father," Clare responded, equally firm and gripping her own bright sword. "Kira will stay with Finn. I will go with you to see about the goblin."

Amias looked from one to the other: Clare, tall and straight, with her flowing silver hair and sky blue eyes; Tomas, with his tanned, wrinkled skin, dark and bent with age. They were very dissimilar in actual appearance, but strikingly the same in their strength of will. He had seen this too many times not to know what was coming. With an ease of habit that now almost seemed like instinct after ten years of marriage, Amias sided with his wife.

"Kira, take Finn inside," he said, smiling as he winked at his daughter. "Be sure to bar the door. Your grandfather, mother and I are going out to assess this goblin situation."

Now you may wonder at the wisdom of Amias leaving his children alone in the house with goblins about, but children learn self-reliance early in farming communities. Due to the vast number of local predators, survival training has long been part of the core curriculum in the county schools.

Kira, eight years old and small for her age, was already an expert swordswoman. She was also skilled with the bow, and had won a blue ribbon in her division at the Surreydale county fair the previous fall.

Finn was only five, and his survival training involved mostly escaping and hiding, but he was exceptionally quick on his feet and had shown a remarkable talent for moving quietly through almost any terrain.

Elven children, whether from nature or nurture, are the best behaved of children. Without a word of protest, Kira took Finn's hand and led him into the house. Amias listened until he heard the bolt slide into place, then he turned to Clare and Tomas.

"Let's go," he said, and they started across the yard.

CHAPTER 3

*T*he elves made no attempt to hide their approach, but elves move so quietly under normal circumstances that Thrax didn't hear them until they were very near. I'm sure somewhere in his pain-wracked mind a flicker of hope burst forth, whispering that he might still take someone with him into the dark unknown.

Now in all the years I knew of him Thrax was many things, but he was never a coward. Well, perhaps that one time, but that incident occurred much later in the story and involved a matter of the heart. In battle, Thrax never lacked courage. In any case, he didn't care to die lying flat on his belly in a dirt field. In spite of his pain and injuries, he managed somehow to raise himself into a more or less sitting position. Baring his teeth, he turned to face the elves.

The moon was behind him, so Amias, Clare and Tomas could only see his silhouette as they approached. They could tell he was wobbling a bit from side to side. Thrax had no weapons, but as the elves drew nearer he began to curse them and swear vengeance on them, promising them all manner of misery if they should only get close enough for him to reach them from where he sat. All this bluster did not affect the elves in the least. They could see that Thrax was severely injured. They knew very well that if he could have stood up, he would already have done so.

The trio stopped within about ten feet of Thrax. He was still cursing, but, to his great mortification, his voice was beginning to falter and he was having more and more difficulty in not toppling over. Finally he had to choose between threatening the elves and breathing. The need for air seemed slightly more pressing, so Thrax stopped swearing and sat panting. He did manage a rather fierce glare, but it only made him seem the more pitiful because there was obviously only a great deal of wishful thinking behind it.

The night was quiet for some time as they studied each other, the elves and the dying goblin. The harvest moon shone down with merciless light, casting the tableau in bas-relief. I'm sure Thrax longed to catch one of the elves so that he could share some of the anger and humiliation he felt, but he seemed finally to accept that he could never reach them and closed his eyes to hide his pain. His body continued to sway unsteadily, but he refused to fall.

"Why don't they just finish it?" he thought angrily, as his life's blood soaked his clothing and his limbs grew cold.

"Can you help him?" Clare was the first of the elves to break the silence and her question was for her husband. Her beautiful face was lined with concern, and pity was in her voice and heart as she watched Thrax sinking lower and lower toward the ground.

"Help him?" roared Tomas. "Help him? I'll help him to the grave! After all they've done!" He shook his head in disgust.

"Father, he's only a child!" Clare exclaimed. "You can't blame him for the actions of others."

"You think he wouldn't kill us if he could?" Tomas shouted. "Daughter, have you lost your mind?"

"He's a child, just a child!" Clare cried, as tears filled her great blue eyes. "He's not a wild beast! The Great Creator…"

"The Great Creator never made the likes of him!" Tomas interrupted angrily. "He has no soul! He's a savage, though he walks upright!"

"And are we no better?" Clare asked, turning on him with sudden fury. "Will we behave as savages, too? Will we murder him here, in this field, without a thought?"

"We'll put him out of his misery," said Tomas. "We'll be doing him a favor," but his voice fell and he couldn't meet Clare's eyes. You see, Tomas was a kindly old elf, although, for right or wrong, he was certainly prejudiced against goblins. Those who knew him well might have considered that he had good reasons even then for feeling the way he did.

"Amias," Clare began, turning to her husband, but Amias seemed unaffected by the heated exchange between father and daughter. His lean brown face was intense, his expression absorbed and, to her great relief, Clare read compassion in his eyes. She had seen this look on her husband's face countless times before. Amias was examining his patient.

Amias Strong was a physician from a long line of physicians. The oath he took on the day of his commencement was woven into the very fabric of his frame. Regardless of what anyone else thought or said, Amias could not let a life, any life, slip away without putting out his hand to try to wrest it from Death's grasp.

"It may be hopeless. I must admit his prognosis seems poor," said Amias absently, almost to himself. "I need to get closer, but I don't think he will like that." He rubbed his chin. "Perhaps some anesthesia...."

"I'll get it!" Clare was moving immediately, pale hair flying as she ran toward the house to fetch her husband's medical bag.

CHAPTER 4

*T*hrax did not wake up the next morning, or the morning after. Three days passed before he opened his bleary green eyes. His surprise was surpassed only by his greater displeasure at finding himself strapped to a rather uncomfortable cot. Lacking any practical life experience that might have kept him silent until he could better assess his current situation, he soon made enough noise to alert the family, and most of their neighbors, to the fact that he was indeed still alive and now awake.

Fortunately the children were at school, because the arrival of Amias and his wife drove Thrax into an even greater frenzy and the words that came from his mouth, well, I wouldn't dare repeat them. Suffice it to say that threats of murder were made and included fairly imaginative descriptions of torture, especially coming from a ten-year-old goblin. He had amazing strength considering his recent brush with death and I'm sure would have turned his bed over had it not been bolted to the floor.

"I'm afraid I shall have to sedate him," Amias said briskly as he opened a drawer in the stand beside the bed. He drew a yellowish liquid into a large syringe and skillfully injected it into Thrax's left shoulder, in spite of his struggling and cursing and trying to bite. The drug worked wonderfully well and within a few moments Thrax was quiet.

"The surgeries saved his life," Amias sighed, "but now I'm not sure what we're going to do with him. His right arm was almost severed and will take months to heal. If he develops infection, he may still lose the arm. He won't be able to survive on his own for a very long time."

"You did the right thing," said Clare, slipping her hand into his, "so only good can come of it."

Amias did not answer. While he greatly admired his wife's faith, he himself couldn't always share her hopeful outlook. He had observed things during the course of his medical career that at one time had made him doubt even the existence of a Creator, much less the active interest of a kindly caring one. In the maturity of his age, he had accepted what he could not understand, recognizing the undeniable presence of a skilled craftsman in the intricacies and miracles of nature. But did the Creator truly care about him or his family? Amias was not sure.

Fortunately, whether through divine intercession or just plain luck, the problem of what to do with Thrax was resolved fairly quickly. You see, whatever you may have heard about the intelligence of goblins, they could not have survived for as long as they have done without being extremely adaptable. When Thrax woke the second time, he had already learned that causing a commotion was not in his best interest. As he lay quietly on his uncomfortable cot, he realized that the elves had not killed him though they could have. Instead they had apparently worked hard to save his life. Regrettably, I must say that this did not in any way illicit the feelings of gratitude one might expect. Instead, Thrax held the elves in great contempt for the weakness he saw in their compassion.

"What a bunch of sheep!" he thought in disgust. "What idiots! Why would they help me? Don't they know I'll kill them?" He had a sudden spark of memory, of words spoken softly in a moonlit field.

"He's only a child." One of them had said that. One of them had said that about him!

"They think I'm just a boy, that I'm weak, that I'm nothing!" He forgot himself in his anger and howled with rage.

"Please don't do that." The voice was soft, musical and merry.

Thrax turned his head on the cot to see Clare entering the room. Clare was tall and fair and she was wearing a soft, flowing dress covered in pale blue flowers. She was, as I have always thought, quite beautiful, but at that time, Thrax couldn't see it or appreciate it in any way. It was her voice, he remembered. She was the one who had called him a child!

"I'll kill you!" Thrax snarled without thinking. "Untie me right now! I'll kill you!"

To Thrax's great surprise and even greater indignation, Clare simply laughed. She pulled a chair next to the head of his cot, sat down and calmly folded her hands in her lap.

"Let's think about this," she said, gazing at Thrax, her left eyebrow raised quizzically. "You want me to untie you and you'll kill me."

She cocked her head to the side.

"Does that sound like a good idea? Now if you asked to be untied so you could help with lunch, or so that you could help with chores, I might consider it. But, no, I won't untie you so you can kill me."

Clare stood up.

"You might want to mull that over a bit." She smiled at him, and then turned and left the room.

Thrax looked after Clare in amazement. He felt stunned and confused, and some of his anger left him. He lay quietly and tried to consider his options. You must remember that Thrax was only ten years old and had very little experience with the world. He had almost died and now was on his own trying to deal with people he couldn't possibly understand. The elves were fools, he thought, but not idiots. They would not untie him from the cot if he threatened them. Clare had made her point. But, what should he do?

Black thoughts overtook him and something like cunning opened the eyes of his mind.

"I will pretend to be grateful that they have saved me," he thought with a sudden flash of inspiration. "They think I'm just a boy. When they least expect it, I'll kill them all in their sleep."

Thrax couldn't help smirking as he lay there plotting the deaths of the elves.

Later that afternoon, Amias Strong strode briskly up the road toward his home. He had been gone all day. His nearest neighbor and dear friend, Jacob Turngood, had sliced through his own leg while chopping wood. The injury was such that Jacob could have bled to death. Luckily he had two stout sons who had carried him into the house and staunched the bleeding while his daughter, Molly, had run for the doctor. Amias was fairly confident that Jacob would recover in time.

Tomas had, as usual, been hard at work at his forge. Tomas was an expert craftsman, the son of craftsmen who for generations had excelled in the making of swords. He took great pride in the intricate yet functional designs of the hilts in addition to the balanced and razor sharp blades. His reputation was such that he had recently been honored by an order for several weapons and the opportunity to construct the royal family's coat of arms for the front hall of the House at Heath Downs, seat of the King of the Eastern Elves, Erron Thornehart.

Kira and Finn had both spent an exceptionally unremarkable day at school.

It was by chance that they all arrived in the front yard at the same time that afternoon and were all shocked, though not to an equal degree, to see Thrax, sitting quietly on the front porch with Clare while she shelled peas for dinner, just as if he had been doing so all of his life.

So began Thrax's association with the Strong family.

That evening Amias explained the extent of his injuries and told Thrax what to expect in the way of recovery. Many of the words Amias used were beyond his comprehension, but Thrax listened carefully and silently. He had already tested his own strength and was sensible enough to realize that without the use of his right arm he would not survive for long in the Wide World. He reluctantly accepted that his plans for murder were not practical in the immediate future, but were something to be looked forward to perhaps in the spring. Until then, he would take advantage of this opportunity to learn all he could about his enemies, or so were his thoughts at the time.

CHAPTER 5

*W*ord of the Strong family's new guest spread through the town with amazing speed. Even though the Strong family was one of the most prominent and respected families in Surreydale, their neighbors were still hard pressed to accept the addition of a goblin, even a young convalescing goblin, to their quiet community. Many had lost livestock and a few had even lost family members or friends to the goblins over the years. Some were more outspoken than others, but it was actually those who said the least that caused Amias the most concern. He was fairly certain that a plot was being developed to dispose of Thrax, and more alarming was his suspicion that his father-in-law was not only aware, but was actively involved in the plan.

Tomas had said very little about and nothing at all to Thrax since the night of the raid. Even his general grumblings seemed subdued, creating a most unusual state of peace in the house and raising Amias' suspicions further. I myself was well aware of the plot, though I gave it little thought. I have my own responsibilities, and though I find the other races intriguing at times, I rarely involve myself in their affairs. I will say that it was fortunate for Thrax that he was too weak at that point to wander far from the house alone.

In the meantime, Clare was busily incorporating Thrax into the household, an extraordinary feat even for someone with Clare's talents. Within a few weeks, Kira and Finn had more or less accepted Thrax and were no longer especially fearful around him. This was quite an accomplishment when you consider that Thrax at ten years of age was as tall as Amias and taller than Tomas.

Besides his height, Thrax had the usual goblin physiology that frightens most children; the angular face and bulging green eyes, the white, wolfish fangs, the grayish green mottling of the skin.

For his part, Thrax had been terribly hurt and continued to have a great deal of pain. He was forced to move slowly and to rest often. He tried hard not to show any weakness in front of the elves, not because he feared them, but because he held them in such utter contempt for saving his life.

Fall crept softy away, only disrupted by one near disaster at the Strong house. It all started with the horses.

CHAPTER 6

While Clare's family had been expert craftsmen, the Strong family, in addition to producing physicians, excelled in the breeding of horses. Intelligent and agile, and with amazing stamina, these horses were like none others ever seen in Surreydale, or anywhere else in the Wide World. Their appearance was no less remarkable than their other qualities. All were snow white, with a lacy blanket of jet black across their flanks and withers that resembled the intricate pattern of a spider's web. Their hooves were the color of obsidian and twice as hard, and their eyes were emerald green. Though elves and men came from far and wide, some bringing exorbitant offers, the horses of the Strong family were never sold. Ownership only passed outside the family by gift.

Thrax had seen the horses from the house, and thought them very interesting. I'm ashamed to say that their beauty and spirit were lost on him. He could not admire them as anything other than as something he might like to eat. In his self-designated role as spy to the elves, he resolved to investigate the horses further.

One afternoon in early November, while Clare was working at her loom and Tomas was at his forge, Thrax decided to satisfy his curiosity by taking a little stroll out to the barn.

As he approached the wide, dimly lit hallway, he could see several horses' heads extending over the stall doors. Most seemed to be lazily chewing wisps of hay and had their eyes half-closed. That is, until they suddenly became aware of Thrax.

In an instant it seemed the entire barn had exploded in clouds of dust and hay as the horses bolted around inside their stalls, neighing wildly. Thrax froze in the open doorway and stared in surprise. He hadn't done anything. Why had the horses gone mad?

Alarmed by the commotion, Tomas came running. Grabbing a pitchfork that was standing by the tack room door, he sprang at Thrax with murderous intent. As you may know, goblins are not agile as a rule and Thrax, being injured, was even less so than usual. He stumbled backward and tumbled to the ground, landing hard on his still healing right shoulder. Grunting in pain, Thrax scarcely had time to raise his left hand to try to ward off the attack as Tomas rushed forward.

"You filthy, sneaking brute!" Tomas spit, plunging the tines of the pitchfork into the dirt as Thrax rolled away, barely avoiding the charge.

"What do you think you're doing out here? You came after the horses, didn't you?"

"What if I did!" snarled Thrax, rolling to the right to escape as Tomas lunged again.

Now you will recall that I said Thrax was not a coward and that he was adaptable. I never said he was particularly wise. Thrax had been doing a fair job of hiding his true nature by keeping his thoughts to himself around the elves, but he was, after all, a goblin. Tomas had barely missed killing him twice and it's certain that he would not miss a third time. Making Tomas more angry was not the smartest thing for Thrax to do under the circumstances.

Thrax grabbed for the handle of the pitchfork, but the old elf was too quick. He jumped back and prepared to shove the tines straight through Thrax's thick chest.

"Father, don't!" Clare gasped as she ran across the yard from the house, her pale hair flying like moonbeams.

Tomas froze and Thrax couldn't help sneering at him. The look on Thrax's face made Tomas raise the pitchfork again, but he didn't strike. Clare ran to his side and grasped his arm.

"Father, what happened?" Concern was in her eyes as she searched his face.

"This aberration of nature was coming after the horses!" Tomas swore, his face dark. He glared at Thrax as he continued. "We should have finished him in the field. We should never have brought him into this house."

"It would have been murder." Clare said simply.

Tomas was silent for a moment. Slowly he lowered the pitchfork and Thrax cautiously sat up.

"You're going to regret this, Daughter. I feel it in my bones. You didn't see what they did to Mariss."

"I'm sorry, Father. I'm sorry about Mariss," she said.

Clare reached out to comfort him, but Tomas put up his hand to wave her away. His wrinkled face seemed to collapse in upon itself and his lip trembled.

"The Great Creator protects those who do his will. Mariss is in a better place," Clare offered hopefully.

"She would have to be," Tomas agreed bitterly, then turned fiercely. "Some place where there are no goblins!" He spat on the ground as he walked away.

Clare lowered her eyes, her beautiful face sad. Then, without a word, she reached out her hand to help Thrax up. It was a delicate hand, but strong. Thrax hesitated for a moment before taking it. His expression was as thoughtful as I have ever seen on a goblin's face. Finally he scrambled up, looking at Clare oddly, as if seeing her for the first time, a question in his dark green eyes.

"You must not bother the horses, Thrax," she said.

"Elven horses know all about goblins. They can recognize you by your scent, even before they see you," she explained as they walked slowly back to the house. "If you are hungry, just let me know. Elves don't eat horses, but I'll be happy to fix you something else."

She sounded so very rational, so unaccountably reasonable that Thrax stopped walking and stared. Clare wasn't criticizing him or condemning him, goblin though he was. She seemed to accept him, maybe even respect him. He staggered slightly and Clare took his arm. To my surprise, Thrax didn't pull away. Instead, I saw him lean on her as he stumbled up the front steps to the porch. I knew then that Clare had captured him, as she had captured us all, not by force, but by the indomitable power of her kindness and strength of her heart.

His shoulder did not suffering any significant injury from the skirmish with Tomas, and Thrax continued to improve. Driven to desperation by the encounter, Tomas sought support from Amias in driving the goblin from the household, but to no avail.

Blessed with an easygoing, though somewhat dispassionate nature, Amias was generally satisfied to let his wife run the family as she chose. Clare was fiery, but extraordinarily sensible, and Amias trusted her judgment regarding most things as much as he trusted his own. Though he respected his father-in-law and was appropriately concerned about his children and his horses, Amias sided with Clare.

CHAPTER 7

*W*inter was exceedingly harsh that year, and all outdoor activities were soon put to an end by recurrent blizzards and ice storms. Without warning, these storms fell like avalanches down the Suraelian Mountains, covering the town in blanket upon blanket of beautiful and treacherous snow. Those elves that kept livestock ran thick cords from their houses to their barns so as not to be caught in the open while tending their cattle, horses or sheep.

It was a difficult time for predators and prey. The goblins that had been hunting elsewhere since the unsuccessful attack by Thrax's troop on Surreydale in the fall came back and lurked in Drae Woods where the snow was less deep. They, along with the wolves and great cats, hunted each other when no other more eligible quarry was available.

Due to the weather, school was suspended and the children worked on their lessons at home. Though he feigned indifference as he sat silently by the fire, Thrax found himself secretly fascinated by some of the subjects Kira studied, especially history and geography. He knew so little of the Wide World and had never thought to think about other people and other lands.

To everyone's astonishment, Thrax was regaining some of the sensation in his right hand, a finding that was quite remarkable especially to Amias.

"The nerves in your arm are regenerating," he told Thrax in surprise. "I've never seen anything like this in any of the higher species. As far as I know only some of the reptiles and amphibians have been shown to have the capacity to re-grow a limb. "

Thrax wasn't sure whether to be honored by his inclusion in the category of "higher species", or insulted by being compared to the lower ones.

Amias showed Thrax some exercises for improving his range of motion and strengthening his grip and Thrax performed them daily. He was still planning to kill the elves and was anxious to be ready by the time spring arrived.

Clare had exciting news for her family that brought some much-needed light to those long, dark days of winter. She was expecting another child. She told Amias first and he announced it to everyone that evening at the dinner table. The joy and celebration that followed had to have warmed even a goblin's heart. I was told that, caught up in the moment, Tomas actually shook hands with Thrax before he realized what he'd done and turned away.

CHAPTER 8

*T*he last great storm came in early March, culling the very young and the very old of most every species that lived on the land. Shortly after, The Thaw began, bringing glimpses of spring and creating new hardships for the denizens of Surreydale. I'm referring to The Floods, of course. As the snow began to melt, what started as a trickle soon became a rushing, swirling, crashing wall of water that cascaded down the mountains, sweeping away anything and everything in its path.

The children had been back in school for perhaps a week, and Thrax found himself feeling somewhat restless. I like to think that he missed them, though he would never have admitted it to himself or anyone else. It was a bright, clear day and he decided to walk out toward the school in the afternoon to scout the area, as he told himself.

When the bell rang, Thrax watched as a multitude of laughing children rushed out the doors of the neat, white schoolhouse and into the cool, fresh air. He stepped back into the hedges and waited until he saw Kira and Finn separating from the throng and heading toward him and the path home.

"Thrax! Thrax!" Finn saw him first and waved excitedly. Finn was always such a pleasant child and had at that time a very trusting nature.

Thrax stepped away from the hedge and approached the

children cautiously. He was accustomed to their presence at home, but even so, rarely spoke to them; and this was the furthest he had come into town since his injury.

Finn ran up to Thrax, but Kira continued unhurried. She neither smiled nor waved. Thrax noticed some of the children in the yard had stopped talking and laughing and were staring at him. He also noticed that Kira kept glancing uneasily over her shoulder.

"Why are you here?" Kira asked, rather curtly, as she joined the two boys.

She clearly was not as pleased to see Thrax as Finn was. Frowning, she gazed back toward the schoolyard. Some of the older boys were standing together, talking intently and watching Thrax. After a moment, one of them jogged off toward town. The others stayed where they were.

Thrax didn't know what to say in answer to Kira's question.

"Why not?" was his less than witty retort.

Kira gave Thrax a stern look, and then took Finn's hand and started down the path. Thrax fell in behind them. He looked back once and observed that the group of boys was no longer standing in the yard.

The path was narrow and lined by brush. It wound along the river Rione on the southwestern border of Surreydale until it reached the forest, then branched to the north and the south. The distance would not have been half so far as the cormorant flies, but due to the winding of the river it was almost three miles from the school to the Strongs' farm.

Kira set a brisk pace, but it was difficult to keep Finn moving. There were signs of spring everywhere, and Finn wanted to stop and examine every insect or animal or budding leaf that caught his eye. Kira was looking about too, but Thrax was fairly certain she was not admiring the flowers. Kira may have heard them, but I am sure Thrax was totally amazed when the older boys from the schoolyard seemed to materialize from thin air, surrounding them and blocking the path.

I was not near enough to hear what was said. One of the taller boys approached Thrax and must have made a rude comment. Before anyone could stop him, Finn kicked the boy in his shin. All the elves leapt on Thrax at once, trying to bear him down, and Finn was lost somewhere in the milieu. Kira shouted and, picking up a stick, attempted to break up the fight. There was a great deal of crashing about in the brush, and staggering and stumbling to and fro. But, as often happens when mobs act without thinking, the innocent are the unintended victims. The next thing anyone knew Finn had fallen, with arms flailing, into the river.

The Rione was high, but had not yet crested, and was two feet below its bank. Finn hit the icy water with a splash and was immediately swept away. Thrax and the elves froze, unable to comprehend what had just happened. Kira shoved one of the boys hard.

"Get help!" she ordered, trying to get the boy moving in the direction of town. Then she grabbed Thrax by the arm.

"We have to catch him before he reaches the bridge!"

Kira started to run, but Thrax just stood there, looking at her incredulously. She turned and called back, "Come on!"

Now in his mind, Finn was already dead and Thrax could see no reason to rush to pull a tiny dead elf from a raging river. He was not particularly hungry, and Finn was too small to make a meal in any case. But Kira's eyes were turning red and tears were starting to stream down her cheeks. Thrax couldn't explain why, but that bothered him. He began to run with Kira down the path.

They could still see Finn, a tiny speck bobbing in the water, but as fast as they ran, the river ran faster. They were more than a mile from home when Kira stopped, panting for breath. She had a small silver whistle that she wore around her neck and she put it to her lips. She waited for a second, and then blew the whistle again. It had a high musical tone, not shrill, but with a clarity that would carry a good distance.

"Let's keep running," Kira said breathlessly, "she'll find us and we can't afford to lose sight of Finn."

Thrax had no idea what Kira meant, but there was no time now for discussion. Though he was tiring, his pride would not allow him to be outdone by a girl, especially an elf. They dashed on quickly along the river. The path was turning toward the Strongs' farm and they could see the bridge appearing faintly on the horizon. From the town, the sound of bells rang through the cool afternoon. One of the boys had sounded the alarm.

As they rounded the next turn, Thrax saw something large and white flashing through the trees from the direction of home.

"Rosie!" Kira shouted, and there was relief and gratitude in her voice.

The mare ran to them and slid to a stop, breathing hard. She snorted through her nose at Thrax, but did not shy away. Kira grabbed Rosie's mane and leapt to her back, then reached out her hand to Thrax.

"Jump up behind me," she said. "It's the only way we'll ever catch Finn."

I almost laughed out loud at the look on his face; not that anyone would have known it was a laugh if I had. As I said, Thrax was no coward. Without a word, he took Kira's hand and swung up on Rosie's back. Then they were off.

Now, as I've mentioned, goblins are not the most agile of creatures and Thrax still had limited use of his right arm. He had never been on a horse before in his life. How he managed to stay on, with Rosie's dodging and lunging through the brush along the river, is still a wonder to me.

The path widened and became more level as they approached the bridge and Rosie stretched into a sprint. She hit the boards at top speed and never slowed until she was in the middle of the span. There she clattered to a halt, and all eyes searched the waters anxiously in both directions for Finn.

"There he is!" breathed Kira, pointing up the river above the bridge. "We made it."

"Now what?" Thrax asked, a bit out of breath himself from the frantic scramble to reach the bridge.

"You jump in and save Finn," Kira replied, with a mildly exasperated look on her young face. "What did you think?"

I think, because Thrax was so very tall, that Kira considered him practically an adult. Besides, her father had saved Thrax's life, and Finn was in trouble because he had tried to defend Thrax. An elf, any elf, would have felt a moral obligation to risk his or her own life to repay such a debt. Unfortunately for Kira, Thrax was a goblin.

"Nuts to that," snorted Thrax as he slid from Rosie's back and started back across the wooden planks. Kira sent Rosie after him and headed him off.

"It's your fault he fell in!" exclaimed Kira. "You have to save him!"

She was starting to cry again in fear and frustration, but she jumped down from Rosie's back and shoved Thrax as hard as she could.

I'm ashamed to say that he laughed at her. She was a

tiny little thing. In the meantime, the Rione was rushing Finn closer and closer to the bridge.

"He's already dead." Thrax laughed again and Kira's face went very white. Her lips pressed together in a thin line. She squared her shoulders and looked Thrax straight in the eye.

"My grandfather was right about you," she said, and her words were as cold as the river. "My father should have let you die."

She held his gaze for a moment, and then turned to Rosie. Jumping on the mare's back, Kira guided the horse quickly from the bridge and headed her down the bank toward the water. Thrax stood where he was, staring after them. Then he looked back. Finn was very near now.

Rosie did not hesitate as she reached the river's edge. She pushed straight ahead into the rushing, swirling waves. But as the ground fell away and she started to swim, she was swept back toward the bank. Again and again she tried. She leapt and she lunged, but it was no use. The current was too strong. Kira looked up to see Finn, crashing through the pilings under the bridge, and she felt her heart stop.

"Finn! Finn!" Kira cried, in her hopelessness and fear.

What prompted him to act? I've never been sure. But at that moment, Thrax dove from the bridge straight into the river, as graceful and as fierce as any bird of prey.

CHAPTER 9

*T*he water was frigid, and the shock of the impact forced the air from his lungs in a great gasp, but Thrax's aim was surprisingly good. He resurfaced almost under Finn, and quickly scooped the elf up as they were swept together by the crushing current.

Finn showed no signs of life, and in that instant Thrax felt he had just made one of the most ill judged decisions of his young life. The urgency of the situation left him no time to consider the rashness of his actions further as he struggled to keep his head above the roiling waves.

From the river, he could not see Kira, nor could he tell which bank was closest. His right arm was still weak and he was using his left to hold Finn. The best he could manage was to kick his feet as he dodged the trees, limbs and other debris that were swirling around him in the churning water.

On the bank, Kira and Rosie were trying to keep pace with Thrax and Finn, but the trees were becoming more dense and their progress was slow. She was so focused on her brother and his plight that Kira failed to notice when the light began to fade. Then the first wolf howled, and the hair on the back of Kira's neck prickled. She looked about anxiously. Rosie snorted and her trim ears shifted back and forth searching for any sounds of movement among the trees. As you know, the woods surrounding Surreydale were home to many predators, any number of whom would have felt fortunate to stumble upon Kira and her mare.

Struggling against her own fear and better judgment, Kira urged Rosie forward, but as the sun set she found she could no longer see her brother or Thrax in the dark waters of the river.

Kira despaired for a moment, thinking they might have both drowned, but then gathered her courage as she remembered a line from a nursery rhyme, one that her grandfather had taught her when her mother wasn't close by to hear: "Werebeasts are wooly and Trolls are all fat, but Goblins have nine lives and eyes like a cat". Thrax had survived the battle with the elves of Surreydale; Kira had to believe he could survive the river.

Rosie came to an abrupt halt and Kira felt her body go rigid. The mare didn't snort. She didn't make a sound. Instead she stood, a starkly white statue, waiting. Kira strained her eyes trying to see through the gathering gloom.

"What is it, girl?" she whispered.

Rosie tossed her head in answer, but stayed where she was, facing southeast, ears pricked forward. Kira listened intently and almost thought she could make out the faint thudding of footpads on the mossy bank, and then the wolves attacked.

They came quietly and in a rush. Kira felt Rosie's strong back tense, and then she reared and plunged toward the nearest wolf, striking out with her forefeet. The wolf dodged too slowly, caught a glancing blow to his shoulder and drew back. Rosie spun as quickly as a cat and lashed out with her hind legs, striking a second wolf with her sharp hooves. It yelped once, and then dropped like a stone. The remaining wolves approached more warily, snarling, and started to circle.

Kira saw to her dismay that there were at least eight or ten of the great shaggy beasts. Rosie pranced and feigned a rush, then spun and kicked at the wolves that tried to move in behind her. Without benefit of saddle or bridle, Kira tangled her fingers in Rosie's thick mane and clung to her neck like a burr.

Now Rosie was a smart old mare and I could see that she was trying, with her feigns and spins, to create an opening toward the path north and home. The wolves, however, were equally cunning and accustomed to working as a pack. They took turns rushing and snapping at her heels, as they sought to drive the mare deeper into the close quarters of the dense tree trunks. Soon they had the elf and the mare surrounded in such a tight circle that Rosie had very little room to maneuver.

One thin grey wolf darted from the shadows and bowed, directly in front of Rosie. As she lunged for him, two other wolves leapt from behind, trying to bring her down. The mare's hindquarters buckled under the weight and she stumbled, hitting one of the trees so hard that Kira was almost thrown off the other side.

Rosie managed to kick one of the beasts, but the other held on and sank his sharp fangs into her flank. A burst of crimson stained her snow-white coat and rivulets of dark red ran down her hind leg. Rosie's eyes rolled in terror and pain and instinctively she bucked, throwing Kira forward and up onto the mare's neck. Kira wrapped her tiny arms and legs around Rosie's neck and held on for dear life.

The situation did not appear promising for Kira and Rosie, and at that point I had almost made up my mind to step in, though, as I told you earlier, I rarely involve myself in the affairs of the other races. Still, Kira was Clare's daughter, and I didn't think I could bear to see Clare suffer her loss. Fortunately, at that moment help arrived, and from a most unexpected source.

CHAPTER 10

*T*he clear sound of hunting horns pierced the darkness; several horns, and nearby. Then the woods were filled with horsemen and arrows rained upon the wolves. One struck the wolf ripping at Rosie's flank and he immediately went limp and slid to the ground. Many wolves fell and the rest scattered as the horsemen advanced.

Among the archers were riders holding lanterns and the shadows fled with the wolves. Kira, struggling to dismount without falling, was caught by a tall young elf dressed in a forest-green hunting cloak. He lifted her to the ground, and then knelt before her.

"My Lady," he said, and his face though young held a sensibility beyond his years, "are you all right? What brings you to these woods, alone and so late at night?"

Kira was trembling from head to toe and found herself unable to speak. She did not know this elf, though there was something familiar about him and he had rescued her from the wolves. But the events of the day would have been overwhelming for an adult and Kira was only 8 years old. She needed her mother, and no one else could comfort her. Kira began to cry in great racking sobs.

"I'm sorry for your distress, My Lady," the youth said, taking both of her small, cold hands in his. "I fear I have caused you more. You do not know me, and I should introduce myself. I am Nolan Thornehart, crown prince and son of Erron Thornehart, king of the Eastern Elves. I pledge myself to your service. Tell me how I may help you."

Well, that's why he looked familiar! I couldn't blame Kira for not knowing him, as I hadn't recognized him myself.

Prince Nolan had traveled with his guards to Surreydale on several occasions to meet with Tomas about his family's coat of arms. He was a noble, though not a very handsome prince; his title more impressive than his person. The children had initially been drawn by his celebrity and excitedly peeped at him from windows and around doors, but Nolan was too solemn and soft-spoken to hold their attention. They soon lost interest and returned to their usual pursuits. I believe his responsibilities, both present and future, weighed heavily upon him even then.

I found it odd that the crown prince should shirk his royal duties to engage in a hunting party purely for pleasure and so far from Heath Downs, until I recalled the rumors of war that had begun to surface throughout the county. Perhaps Prince Nolan was hunting for more than wild game in Drae Woods.

"I...I...Your Highness..." began Kira, somewhat heartened by this offer of assistance from so renowned a person, "my horse, Rosie, she's hurt."

"Cormac," Nolan called, looking around as a short, stocky elf with curly, black hair rode forward into the light. "Please see to this young lady's horse."

"Of course, Sir," replied the steward, dismounting and turning immediately to Rosie.

Rosie did not shy away as Cormac approached. Lacking the more evolved attributes of worry or regret, Rosie had dismissed the wolves almost as soon as they had disappeared into the forest. She was in some pain, but it was not severe, and she had no reason to expect unkind treatment from elves in general or Cormac in particular.

"It's not too bad, Sire," Cormac reported cheerfully, after examining Rosie for a moment. "She'll be fine and fit in no time at all."

He gave Rosie a drink from his water bottle, pulled a nosebag from his saddlebags and filled it with grain, then placed it over Rosie's head. As she munched, he went to work cleaning the wound on her flank.

"Now," said Nolan, drawing Kira's attention from her mare, "who are you and what are you doing here?"

He led her to a nearby tree root, gnarled and rising from the earth, and they both sat down. Kira brushed at her sleeve and smoothed her skirt. She had dressed appropriately for school that day, not for chasing about on horseback or for fighting wolves; no more was she prepared to meet a prince.

"My name is Kira Strong," she began. "My father is Amias Strong and my grandfather is Tomas Keane of Surreydale. I'm here because of Thrax, our stupid goblin." Kira wrung her hands.

"You see, Your Highness, Thrax got in a fight with the kids at school, though that part wasn't really his fault, but if he hadn't come to school, none of this would have happened. Anyway, my brother, Finn, tried to help him but fell into the river, so I whistled for Rosie and we raced to the bridge. Thrax said Finn was already dead, and I got mad, but then Thrax finally jumped in after him, and I was following with Rosie, but it got dark and the wolves came and now I've lost them both."

Kira sighed heavily for emphasis. She had stopped crying. Nolan was a prince and Kira expected, though perhaps unreasonably, that he could somehow solve all of her problems.

For his part, Nolan was more than a little concerned after hearing Kira's disjointed tale. He vaguely remembered being introduced to the Strong children, but had not given them much thought during his subsequent visits to Tomas's forge. Nothing about Kira had seemed particularly amiss at the time, but, due to her highly improbable story, he now feared that she might not be right in her mind. Perhaps she had wondered from her family and become lost in the woods. Nolan was thoughtful for a moment, and then he stood and took Kira's hand. He bowed.

"It's very late, My Lady, and it would be almost impossible to find your brother and your," Nolan hesitated only a fraction of a second, "goblin in the dark. I think we should locate your parents and organize a search party to start out in the morning."

Kira agreed.

"Yes," she said, "I think you are right, Your Highness. Thank you so much for helping me," and she curtseyed and bowed low.

CHAPTER 11

While Kira was busily making the acquaintance of the crown prince of the Eastern Elves, Thrax was struggling to keep his head and Finn's above the dark, churning waters of the Rione. He had managed to secure Finn across his shoulder with the use of his belt, leaving both arms free to push aside limbs and other debris that had been swept down the mountainside with the melting snow.

Thrax learned quickly that trying to swim across the current was a waste of energy, so he took to floating as much as possible on his back. The current had by then carried them many miles downstream and still the force of the river showed no signs of abating. The water was icy cold, cold enough to kill a man or an elf, but goblins can tolerate a wider range of temperatures than most of the races.

As the Rione rounded a sharp bend toward the east, its momentum sent waves crashing against the bank on the west before turning back into the channel and rushing away south to Loch Donla. Thinking this might be his one chance Thrax forced his stiff right arm into action and struck out toward the west, swimming with all of his strength.

The bank was muddy, slippery and steep, but Thrax somehow managed to crawl from the water and drag himself up to drier ground. I say drier because he came up into the Bluefield Marsh, about 50 miles south and west of Surreydale and on the opposite side of the Rione. He had, of course, no idea where he was, only that he had finally escaped the river. Had he believed in a deity, I'm quite sure he would have offered thanks.

Thrax unbound Finn from his shoulder and laid him on the ground. Slumping down beside him, he examined the elf closely. Finn's body felt cold and his skin was pale. Thrax nudged him with the toe of his boot. Finn didn't move.

"Damn!" said Thrax, "Damn!" He scowled at Finn. "Stupid little elf," he muttered under his breath.

It was warmer out of the water but, with wet clothing, still uncomfortably cool. Thrax sighed. He was exhausted and very hungry. As you might expect, he gave serious thought to making a meal, or at least a snack, of Finn; but after all his efforts to save the elf, he didn't feel exactly right about it. Somehow that would have made his leap from the bridge and struggles in the river seem less heroic in his own mind, and he really felt he would have been a hero if only Finn hadn't already been drowned.

Rising stiffly, Thrax looked around. The night was dark, the moon only in its first quarter, but Thrax could distinguish the ancient willows, clumps of swamp grass and faintly luminescent patches of fog that surrounded the hillock where he stood. Though, as with all goblins, his night vision was extraordinary, Thrax could see no better shelter in the immediate area than the one he had.

He wasn't sure where to go, now that he had left the elves. He expected they would blame him for Finn's death, though he himself would argue that it wasn't his fault. He had not started the fight with the school children after all. He had not pushed Finn into the river. He had attempted to save Finn at great personal risk, but Thrax doubted even Clare would understand this time. He was too tired to travel in any case.

A large rotting willow trunk, hollowed out by beetles and then other animals digging for beetles, seemed to offer the most readily available cover, so Thrax crawled inside. It was quite cozy, but spacious enough for him to lie down with his knees curled up. He looked out at Finn's tiny body lying in the open, a tragic figure in the dim light. I can't say Thrax felt grief for the loss of Finn. I think he was more concerned that Finn's body might attract unwelcomed visitors. For whatever reason, Thrax shortly clambered out of his makeshift cave, picked up Finn's body, and carried it back inside with him.

His dreams were troubled and troubling. In one, he fell from a bridge and was immediately swallowed by a huge serpentine monster. Inside the monster were winding tunnels lined with decomposing corpses, some of which looked like Finn. They gaped at him with empty eyes and reached for him with skeletal fingers as Thrax ran faster and faster.

From out of nowhere, Clare was with him. Her beautiful face was lined with sorrow and she looked at Thrax with her sky blue eyes.

"Please," she whispered, "Please help me."

Thrax reached for her hand, but when he touched her, her entire body shattered into bright splinters of glass that ripped through his body as they fell. He looked down at his own hands and was overcome by horror as he saw they were covered with blood.

Thrax woke in a cold sweat. What he saw when he opened his eyes made him question whether he wasn't still trapped in his nightmare world. Finn's body had been moved. It was lying on its side facing Thrax and Finn was looking straight at him. For a moment, Thrax was frozen in place, trying to understand. And then, Finn blinked.

Thrax started to laugh, not in humor, almost in hysteria. He sat up and reached to touch Finn's hand. It was warm! Finn sat up, stretched his arms and looked around.

"Where are we?" he asked.

Thrax struggled to control the urge to laugh again.

"We're lost," Thrax said, grinning oddly.

Thrax's answer, coupled with his expression, was obviously disturbing to Finn, who frowned. Finn was short enough to stand within the willow trunk, and so he did. He brushed off his pants and peered out the opening. It was still dark, but the sky in the East was growing lighter.

"Did you fall into the river, too?" Finn asked, turning back to Thrax.

"Nope...didn't fall...jumped...from the bridge..." Thrax shook his head in the negative and then nodded his head up and down so many times that Finn was reminded of a toy he had received on his last birthday. It was a miniature marionette whose head, arms and legs jerked when you pulled its strings.

"You jumped in to save me?" Finn's face brightened in surprise. He beamed at Thrax, and then he threw his tiny arms around the goblin's neck. "I knew we were friends!"

Finn stepped back and smiled, and then he punched Thrax in the shoulder with his tiny fist. Thrax, feeling more than a little awkward with this effusive display of emotion, sat there looking uncomfortable. Now Thrax would never have admitted that he felt any real affection for the elf at that point, but I do suspect he was secretly glad he had not killed Finn by trying to eat him when he thought Finn was already dead.

CHAPTER 12

*B*ack in Surreydale, rescue parties were forming to begin the search for Finn at first light. Prince Nolan and his soldiers had met with Amias, Clare, Tomas and some of the townsfolk while returning Kira to her home during the night. The story of Thrax and the schoolyard fight was told in a more coherent and convincing manner by the adults and Nolan, though surprised by this confirmation of Kira's unlikely tale, was eager to help.

The prince divided his men among the groups of townsfolk, but kept his personal guard, including the warrior Cathmor and his chief advisor Caedmon with him. Amias, Clare and Tomas also split up, to improve the odds that at least one member of the family might be with the party that located Finn.

Tomas had been devastated by the loss of the children, convinced the whole thing was a plot by Thrax to kill them both. Though Amias and Clare tried to alleviate some of his fears, in spite of their own more rational ones, Tomas had been beyond reason.

"I knew that goblin would get them. I knew it," he repeated over and over to anyone that would listen. When they found Kira with the prince, alive and well, Tomas broke down and sobbed like a child.

The old elf revived somewhat, and Kira was delighted, when Prince Nolan recounted her bravery in the battle with the wolves. She was both embarrassed and flattered when he called her "My Lady, Kira" and I could see that she was quite taken with him.

Her new and childishly romantic feelings for Nolan couldn't compete however with her loyalty to her grandfather, so that morning she was determined to take her place riding behind Tomas in whichever search party he chose. As reward for her selflessness, Tomas, of his own accord, chose to ride with the prince.

CHAPTER 13

As the rescue parties were setting out from Surreydale, Thrax and Finn were picking their way carefully along the west bank of the Rione. The Bluefield Marsh is a dangerous, albeit beautiful place, taking its name from the scores of violet-blue flowers that grow over and camouflage its treacherous quagmires.

It is not without inhabitants, though those that it does have tend to slither. Many of them are reptilian and have very long tongues adapted to snatching from the air the insects and brightly colored birds attracted by the pretty blossoms. The bogs are warm from the decomposition of plants and animals, and a luminescent fog clings to the air above them almost year round.

Though neither Thrax nor Finn had seen or heard of the Bluefield Marsh before, the two wanderers instinctively knew to skirt the softer ground, but progress was slow. As the day wore on, they grew weary and with fatigue came inattention. Thrax was the first to experience the unpleasant sensation of slipping into one of the sinkholes. Finn was much more careful of his feet. Thrax waded right in and was up to his knees before he realized the seriousness of his situation. No one living has measured the depths of the marsh, but the unwary have found it bottomless, at least in the few moments it took them to descend into dark death.

On recognizing his danger, Thrax threw himself backward, grasping for solid ground. Finn rushed forward to help. Had he had the use of both arms, Thrax would have been free in an instant, but his right arm was still weak. The bog sucked resolutely at his legs and even with Finn pulling at his collar Thrax was only able to slow his downward progression by minutes, not hours.

Finn maintained his hold on Thrax's shirt, while looking about desperately for a way to save his friend. Both were too engrossed in the immediate struggle for survival to notice the soft, rasping sound of the mandibles of the Guapo Bog Beetle as it scuttled up behind them. Finn turned at the last possible moment and almost fell into the marsh himself as the beetle charged.

Oddly enough, as soon as Finn looked directly at the giant bug, it stopped and sat very still, apparently trying to blend in with its surroundings. Its color was nondescript and it would have been almost invisible, had it not been for the intermittent blink of its multifaceted eyes.

"What is it? What is it?" demanded Thrax, more angry than afraid. He was sinking in a mud hole and resented the distraction, whatever it might be. He twisted at the waist and glared over his shoulder, but could not see what the commotion was about.

"Some kind of big bug," Finn answered. "It looks dangerous," he added.

"A bug!" exclaimed Thrax. "Well swat it, squash it, do something!"

"I don't have anything to swat it with and my foot's not big enough to squash it." Finn replied, looking down at his feet.

The beetle was almost 6 feet tall, or long, depending on how you measured it. As soon as Finn took his eyes off the Guapo beetle it inched forward.

Finn looked up quickly and frowned. "It's trying to sneak up!" he said, his young voice accusing. "It doesn't move when I'm looking at it."

The beetle sat and blinked.

"Well you can't just stand there and watch it," said Thrax testily. "I'm sinking!" The water was almost up to his hip.

"Maybe I can chase it around in front of you so you can see it," said Finn, scratching his head, "and then you can tell me what to do about it."

He cautiously approached the Guapo beetle, but the bug didn't move. Apparently Guapo Bog Beetles are resistant to being chased by small elves. Finn stamped his tiny foot at the bug and waved his arms. Still it sat and blinked. Then, apparently assessing the situation to its satisfaction, it deliberately extended its long, spiny proboscis.

"It's trying to lick me!" Finn exclaimed, his voice rising as he jumped back. The bug inched forward.

"Damn and damn!" muttered Thrax. "Get around in front of me. Just come around in front of me!" he ordered impatiently.

Finn carefully worked his way around Thrax, keeping his eyes on the bug as he felt with his hands for solid ground. The beetle crept closer until it finally entered Thrax's field of vision. He was surprised at its size, no doubt, but only scowled at it as it flicked its spiny tongue in and out.

The beetle became aware that Thrax could now see it and immediately stopped. It sat and blinked, but only for a moment. Then carefully it extended its tongue and licked Thrax quickly right across the face. Thrax didn't flinch, his scowl only deepened as his green eyes took on an eerie glow. An idea struck him and he kept his hands down.

"You watch the bug," Thrax told Finn. "I'll look away; let it come for me."

"No!" cried Finn. "You already saved me once! I have to help you this time!"

"You will," said Thrax. "Just watch the bug."

"But..." said Finn.

"Watch it!" snarled Thrax, turning his cold green eyes on Finn. The tiny elf went immediately silent and Thrax looked down into the sinkhole.

The Guapo Bog Beetle scuttled quickly forward, obviously anticipating an early dinner. It wrapped its spiny proboscis around Thrax's head and opened its gaping maw, leaning over to grasp Thrax by the shoulders with its forefeet.

Finn gasped, as Thrax remained motionless. The mandibles were inches away, clicking softly as the bug slid them rapidly over each other, honing them to a fine edge. Saliva was dripping down Thrax's neck: a thick, foul ooze. Still, he didn't move.

The bug leaned closer, closer...

Then with savage fury, Thrax reached up with both hands, grasped the beetle's tongue at its root and yanked with all his might. The bug reared back in pain and surprise, pulling Thrax up with it. The rough surface of its tongue provided good traction and Thrax held on, giving the proboscis another yank.

The Guapo struggled frantically to escape, thrashing and leaping about on the ground. Then, opening the hard shell of its back, it extended great opaque black wings that sent the fog swirling as they vibrated rapidly. The beetle began to rise into the air.

Thrax held fast, and for a moment it seemed he might be ripped in two between the force of the bug's ascent and the deadly grip of the sinkhole. In its desperation to flee the pain of its tongue being torn from its mouth, the Guapo proved the stronger. With a sudden lurch, Thrax felt the last vestiges of the swamp slipping from around his ankles as he was pulled into the air. He forced his toes up to keep from losing his boots, and then kicked as hard as he could as soon as he was free.

"Let go!" Finn cried. "You're out! Let go!"

Thrax held fast. It was not that he physically could not let go of the Guapo; it's that, being a goblin, he would not.

This vile bug had attacked him in the most cowardly manner while he was practically, or supposedly, defenseless. I have found that many of the races apply a double standard in judging such behavior. Revering craftiness and duplicity, and placing no value at all on honor in their own dealings, goblins are, nevertheless, outraged by perceived dishonor in others and have, as you are no doubt aware, an insatiable thirst for revenge.

Thrax kicked his feet and yanked at the beetle's tongue, trying to bring it down. The bug could easily lift something of Thrax's weight, but was not accustomed to flying with living, struggling prey hanging from its mandibles. It lost altitude as it shifted from left to right, unable to maintain its balance.

The beetle dipped down, and as Thrax's feet touched the ground he sprang up, shoving his fists into the Guapo's maw with such force that his hands went through the roof of its mouth and straight into its pea-sized brain. A shudder ran through its entire body as the momentum carried the Guapo higher. Then beetle and goblin came crashing to the earth, the bug writhing in its death throes.

Leaping free, Thrax threw himself upon the prostrate Guapo, beating it with his fists, as it rolled onto its back, legs trembling and curling.

"Stop it!" Finn yelled, grabbing Thrax by the shirttail. "It's dead! Okay? It's dead."

Thrax paused only long enough to shove Finn backward, and then continued to pound as the bug's exoskeleton shattered.

Finn landed hard, and for a moment looked as if he would cry. Sitting up, he blinked rapidly, and then slowly clambered to his feet. As he brushed at his pants, an expression crossed Finn's young face that made him look a great deal like Tomas. He marched back to stand beside the fallen bug.

"Aw," he said, frowning, "you're making all its insides come out. It's getting all over you.

Thrax didn't slow his assault, but did glance down at his boots. They were covered in mud from the sinkhole and ooze from the Guapo.

"Aw," said Finn, "it's so nasty! I bet the smell will never wash off."

Thrax took a deep breath. The bug's odor was appalling, even by goblin standards. He stopped suddenly and backed away, wrinkling his nose. Putting his hands on his legs he slowly lowered himself to his knees, and then sat back on his heels. He looked at Finn.

"You think it's dead?" he asked. His voice was soft and oddly calm; the question bizarre in the aftermath of the violence he had just inflicted.

"Yes, I do." Finn nodded, as a watchful expression crossed his child's face.

"You think it stinks?"

"I know it stinks."

"You think I stink?" Thrax narrowed his goblin eyes to slits and glared at Finn.

"Well..." Finn hesitated.

"You think I stink?" Thrax's voice rose threateningly as he stood and towered over Finn, his hands on his hips.

"Well..." Finn looked about quickly, choosing his path of escape. "Yeah. You do."

With that Finn began to run as fast as his short legs would carry him, scrambling through the swamp grass and muck. Thrax lumbered after him, gaining rapidly as he covered in one stride the distance Finn covered in three. Anyone watching would have been assured of the final outcome of so desperate a race: the tiny elf dodging and leaping through the bog, the giant, hulking goblin hot on his trail.

Thrax caught Finn of course, but what happened next, well, it wasn't what you might have expected at all.

Grabbing Finn from behind, Thrax lifted him from the ground, and then spun around and threw him up into the air. Finn, with his hair flying, reflecting gold in the light of the setting sun, squealed in delight. Thrax caught him and tossed him up again, laughing, too.

It was not the same sound he had made when he first discovered Finn was alive. It was a deep, hearty, booming laugh such that no goblin before had probably often made. There was good humor and happiness in his laughter, happiness that Finn was alive, happiness that he had escaped the sinkhole, happiness that the Guapo was dead, happiness to be lost who knew where with no one but a funny little elf for company.

As darkness fell, they continued on their way. Finn jumped up and tried to punch Thrax playfully in the shoulder, but due to his short stature could only reach as high as the goblin's elbow. Thrax returned the gesture, hitting Finn solidly in his shoulder and almost knocking him to the ground as they headed toward the North Star and home.

CHAPTER 14

*F*inn had been missing for seven days and the searchers were looking decidedly grim. Kira continued to ride with her grandfather and he with the prince, as they carefully combed the west bank of the Rione for any signs of elf or goblin. On the east bank, Amias and Clare were searching as well, though there was no way for the groups to communicate across the vastness of the river.

"Do not lose hope," Nolan smiled encouragingly to Tomas, but even the prince's young face showed signs of strain. He knew the chances of finding Finn alive were becoming slimmer and slimmer with each passing day.

"I cannot thank you enough, Your Highness, for joining in this effort. I know you have many more important things to do than to search for one lost child," Tomas said.

"How could I claim to care for my people if I could ignore the plight of even one child?" Nolan answered.

I thought that was a remarkable sentiment from an elf of only twenty, but Nolan proved to be remarkable in many ways that weren't obvious at first glance.

As they rode out in silence, Tomas stayed close by the prince's side. Cathmor took the point position, as was his custom. Caedmon rode on Nolan's left, his aged countenance expressionless, and his sharp eyes watchful.

When the searchers stopped for lunch, Tomas and Kira sat a little apart from the rest of the group. Though each in their own way found comfort in the presence of the prince, neither felt entirely at ease in the company of his guards. Most were battle-hardened veterans, making me question anew the true purpose behind Prince Nolan's visit to the area.

As Tomas and Kira quietly nibbled stale bread and cheese, Nolan approached and sat down.

"How do you fare, My Lady Kira?" he asked politely, but his eyes were drawn to Tomas. The stress of losing Finn had drawn new lines in the old elf's already wizened face.

Kira, young and resilient, filled with her mother's positive attitude, beamed at the prince with resolute hope.

"I am well, Your Highness. I feel sure we will find Finn today."

The conviction in her voice seemed to both cheer and disturb Nolan. He must have marveled that an eight-year-old child could bear the privation associated with a seven-day trek through the woods without complaint, but I'm certain his heart shrank in fear at the thought of how she would react if her brother weren't found, or perhaps worse, if he were found too late.

Tomas looked at the prince, his eyes red-rimmed and hard. His words, unspoken, hung in the air. Tomas was without hope, his own conviction that they would not find

Finn, at least not alive, as firmly fixed as Kira's faith that they would.

"My Lady," Nolan said, "would you do me a great favor? Will you go ask Sloan for my water skin? I have left it hanging from my saddle."

Kira may or may not have seen through this ploy to secure her absence. Eager to please the prince, she leapt to her feet and hurried away on her errand.

"You do not share your granddaughter's optimism." It was a statement. I am certain the prince did not intend to pry. He merely sought to offer comfort through understanding the source of Tomas's pain.

"My grandson..." Tomas shook his head slowly, "The boy is dead. We may as well turn back now. Kira has never seen what a goblin can do." He paused and rubbed his withered hands over his face. "She doesn't know what they did."

Nolan sat in silence, waiting. In the cool stillness of the day, dappled sunlight flooded the clearing around them, but seemed unable to penetrate the darkness in the old elf's face and heart. Instead the light was reflected from him and fled into the shadows of the trees.

"She was special, Mariss was." Tomas whispered at last. "Everyone loved her. Everyone."

"She was my little sister, my only sister, and she had a lot of spirit, but she had a kind heart," his voice grew stronger, "and I used to tease her, well, you never saw the like. But she understood that that was just my way. We understood each other, Mariss and I."

"She knew you loved her in spite of the teasing," Nolan said.

"I think she knew," Tomas agreed softly. "I think she did."

"Where is she now?" Nolan asked, though he, of course, must have known the answer. He could see the pain in Tomas's face, and hear the bitterness in his voice.

"My daughter, Clare, says she's in a better place." He closed his eyes. "I don't know if I believe that."

"I'm sorry," said Nolan, reaching over and grasping the old elf's arm. "I'm sorry for your loss."

"I didn't lose her." Tomas opened his eyes wide as anger crept into his voice. "It was the Goblins. The Goblins took her."

I have often wondered at the effects death and distance have on the memory of a loved one. As Tomas told his story, I reflected on what I had known of Mariss. Raven-haired, with crimson cheeks and eyes of the deepest violet, the Mariss of my memory had not been particularly kind hearted.

Obstinate and headstrong even as a child, she was more like a fairy than an elf, with a beauty that garnered her a great deal of latitude within both her family and the community. Mariss was only seventeen when she met her fate, a fate that, despite her faults, she surely didn't deserve.

You see, Mariss was the youngest and a girl, the sixth child born into an artisan's family prided for working the forge. Doted on by her parents and subjected to relentless ridicule by her five brothers, she learned early that compliance is often perceived as weakness and an agreeable nature is more often imposed upon than it is prized. Consequently Mariss determined to be what Tomas called spirited; others not so charitable might have chosen a much less flattering term.

As she approached the age of consent, many of the young elves she had fought and played with as a child sought to gain her interest to no avail. Mariss seemed to have a special aversion to the complicated interactions the elves called "courting", often rebuffing potential suitors with unconcealed disdain, that is, until she chanced to meet a handsome young elf from Highborough upon Rione.

Highborough upon Rione was a densely populated settlement thirty miles north of Surreydale, home to the only university in the county. Its residents earned their living by engaging in Commerce and spent their leisure time pursuing cultural activities involving The Arts. Compared with Surreydale, Highborough upon Rione was quite the metropolis; the rustic farmers of Surreydale and their families deemed the denizens of Highborough sophisticated and therefore fascinating.

As I mentioned, Mariss had extraordinary beauty, and as many a less attractive female of almost any race will tell you, amiability is not a quality often sought by the young. The Highborough elf took one look at her and was captivated by her loveliness. His polished manners and elegance of speech succeeded where her comparatively ingenuous neighbors could not; our haughty maiden at last succumbed to the allure of love.

She and the Highborough elf were soon inseparable. Where one went, the other followed. They began sneaking off together at inappropriate times and were caught in inappropriate places, much to the dismay of their respective and respectable families. They were forbidden to see each other, which, as you might expect, had the contrary effect of what was intended.

One night in early May, Mariss slipped out to meet her friend and in her haste took an ill-advised shortcut through the woods by the river. You are no doubt by now aware that in a community such as Surreydale the consequences of foolishness, even one small slip in watchfulness, can be dire.

Goblin raiders caught her and, though she fought fiercely, made short work of her. Those of you who know goblins will be assured her death was neither painless nor quick. In the course of the search the following morning, Tomas was the one who found her, or what there was left of her. He was never the same.

As Tomas finished his story, I noticed that Kira had returned and was standing just outside the clearing. She must have overheard much of the tale, as her bright face turned dark.

When Tomas stopped speaking, and before Nolan could offer sympathy or comment, Kira hurried forward and joined them. She handed the prince his water skin without a word and sat so close to her grandfather that no separation in their shadows could be seen.

CHAPTER 15

*T*he elves had set up camp in the narrow tree line along the west bank of the Rione. They were by then 25 or 30 miles south of the wooden bridge. To the west of the river, the grasslands ran parallel to the trees, stretching north toward the Carrick Mountains and Heath Downs, south to the Bluefield Marsh and the Lowland Fens surrounding Loch Donla and west to the craggy ridges of Mount Mourne.

To the east, Drae Woods cradled the southeastern border of Surreydale, extending from the east bank of the Rione all the way to the foothills shadowed by the lofty peaks of the Suraelian Mountains. All within was considered the realm of the Eastern elves, though few traveled through and even fewer inhabited the territory south of Cross Corners, which some may recall as the outpost that lay in the valley between the Carrick Mountains and Mount Mourne.

Watch fires glowed like earthbound stars mingled among the trees and out into the grasslands, marking the borders of the searchers' de facto and defensible, though temporary, shelter. The prince had considered long before allowing the fires to be set. The watch fires served two purposes: they gave notice that a sizable Elven force was in the neighborhood, and they might, with luck, provide a poor lost child a beacon home. They could also, however, draw attention where it was not wanted, that being the basis for Nolan's concern.

It was during the third watch of the night, on the thin, grey cusp of dawn where the boundaries between dreaming and wakefulness blur and the creations of nightmare strive fiercely for manifestation in the factual world, that a tiny, ragged, exhausted creature stumbled into the outer perimeter of the camp. Nolan was first from his bedroll, with Kira close behind him when the shout went up from the sentry.

"What is it, Your Highness?"

Her face was wan in the clinging darkness and she clutched her blanket close about her shoulders in defense against the morning chill.

"I will find out, My Lady." Nolan was unfailingly calm, his presence, reassuring. "Please, wait here."

Unsheathing his sword, the prince strode to the edge of the clearing. Those soldiers that had been sleeping in the camp drew their weapons and melted silently into the tree line. Caedmon stood beside Kira, his ancient blade in hand.

A babble of voices rose in excitement and the light from torches merged and grew brighter as the watchmen rushed together and advanced through the trees. Tomas stumbled stiffly from his bed and stood trembling, his eyes red and bleary, his hand on Kira's shoulder, though for her support or his I couldn't say.

More lights flashed and raced through the trees and the babble rose to an unintelligible din. Kira felt as if her heart must leap from her chest and excitedly squeezed her grandfather's hand. At last the watchmen reached the edge of the clearing and stopped. A short, powerful figure separated from the throng, stepped forward and bowed.

"Your Highness."

The combined torchlight had attained the intensity of a small sun, forcing Nolan, Tomas and Kira to shade their eyes as they squinted, trying to identify the speaker. It was Renny, one of the youngest of the guards.

"Your Highness." His voice rose and then broke with emotion. "The little elf, he's come home."

For a moment I thought he would weep, but being a soldier he could not. The guard fell back, quiet now, their battle-worn faces softened by wonder as they created an opening to the nucleus of the light. At the center of the torchlight stood the great warrior Cathmor, and on his strong shoulders rode the pale but triumphant Finn.

CHAPTER 16

While the elf search party engaged in joyous celebration, a dimmer, less promising sun was peering over the horizon about a mile or so to the south.

Pale tendrils of light sifting through the hazy morning brought little to cheer Thrax as he trotted doggedly along the creek bed. He, like Finn, had been running all night, fleeing the same foe and the promise of death.

Turning northwest, Thrax cut across the rivulet and headed into the brush for several hundred yards, stamping down the grass and breaking twigs haphazardly as he went. Retracing his steps, he re-entered the stream and turned east, sliding his feet through the edge of the water as quietly as he could, trusting it would lead him to the river. Finn had convinced him that their best hope of help would be found there.

"If I was an elf..." he thought, but of course he was not. Cautiously, clumsily, Thrax crept onward in a seemingly futile effort to throw his pursuers off his trail. The stones in the stream were slippery with moss, making each step he took a hazard for falling, for being heard, for being caught.

You'll no doubt be surprised to learn that, during the course of their travels together, Thrax had developed what might be called an almost brotherly regard for Finn, or as near such a feeling as a goblin can mount. Fantastic I know, but nevertheless, I assure you it was so.

Finn, open, artless, and ceaselessly cheerful, had made their journey through the marsh seem less like two retched souls lost in a treacherous wilderness and more like two hale companions on a camping expedition for fun. Thrax, still young and impressionable, could not help but be infected by Finn's good humor; that is until the pair happened upon a den of goblins, ostensibly far from where any goblin might be expected to be.

The goblins had been less pleased with this meeting than either Thrax or Finn, if that were possible. They zealously abused Thrax, as goblins are wont to do with young males of their species: snarling, rushing at him and boxing his ears. At Finn's suggestion, Thrax had pretended the elf was his captive in order to improve his standing and facilitate their escape, but once the charade was exposed, the goblins had given chase. The two had been forced to separate.

Thrax thought briefly of Finn now, hoping he had in fact found safety, though not having time to dwell on the tiny elf's possible whereabouts. As I said, the goblins, at least some of them, were still following him and he, for his life, could not understand why.

True, he had tricked them, and that had made them angry, but he had managed to elude them for almost three days. Though eager and relentless killers, the average goblin has a relatively short attention span and is easily distracted from prey that evades it. Thrax had no idea why this particular group of goblins was so determined to catch him, but of course he could have had no conception then of what was to come.

You see, Thrax and Finn, in their search for a way home, had stumbled quite by accident onto the very fringes of Maelstrom's army.

The rumors of war that had most likely drawn Prince Nolan to Drae Woods had, as so many rumors do, a basis in fact. Maelstrom was marshalling an army. His immediate purpose was to conquer and enslave the elves. His reasons for doing so were known only to himself; I don't believe for a moment that even his closest advisors were then privy to the true motives and plans of the Goblin Lord.

CHAPTER 17

*T*he merrymaking in the elves' camp had subsided. Runners had been dispatched to locate the various search parties and share with them the good news that Finn had been found. Exhausted by his ordeal and overtaxed by the excitement of his rescue, Finn had spoken little, but had eaten ravenously and then crawled into a bedroll. Kira sat beside him, watching over her brother while he slept.

The elves wandered about the camp, speaking softly so as not to disturb the sleeping child, obviously delighted at the unexpectedly happy conclusion of so doubtful a quest and eager to return home; but the prince felt it best to allow Finn at least a few hours rest before starting the long trek back to Surreydale. All was peace seasoned with thankfulness, and then the goblins attacked.

These were not the young, inexperienced goblins of the Surreydale skirmish, though they struck boldly and unexpectedly in the middle of the day. They were not equipped as the usual nomadic raiders with bludgeons or sticks. These goblins brandished halberds and iron-tipped pikes. They wore armor made of thick squares of lacquered leather and carried shields of solid oak. Torques of electrum surrounded their massive necks, and their faces were painted with blood.

They struck with all the savagery for which goblins are known, but with a cold precision and uncharacteristic unity that caught the search party completely unawares. Had it not been for the presence of Prince Nolan's guard, the entire camp would have been annihilated in minutes. As it was, many elves were injured or killed in the ferocity of the initial onslaught.

Renny was one of the first to fall, his head split by a battleaxe wielded by a goblin twice his size. Crying out, the warrior Cathmor struck the goblin down, but too late to save the young soldier.

Two more goblins charged, and for a moment Cathmor disappeared in a whirlwind of dust; but then he reappeared, throwing the goblins back, severing one's head with a single stroke and impaling the other under the arm where the armor failed to cover its wearer. Grabbing a pike from one of his lifeless foes, Cathmor turned and launched it into the broad back of a goblin that held Shanley by the throat, piercing the goblin through.

Still it seemed for every goblin slain, two more appeared in its place. Though the elves fought valiantly, the shear size and number of their enemies drove them back toward the center of the camp and the river. Then three great goblins broke through the line of defenders and assailed Prince Nolan in the clearing of trees. Nolan had helped Finn and Kira up into the mossy branches of a giant oak and would not give ground as he defended his charges.

Tomas and Caedmon, both weathered old elves that had survived many battles, fought at his side.

As the goblins rushed forward, the horses in their terror broke free. Young Cormac tried to calm them, but was caught in the tether rope, dragged through the tree line along the river and then out into the open field. Only Kira's mare Rosie resisted, finally breaking her halter and turning back toward the fray.

Probably by now you are wondering what had happened to Thrax. You may have guessed that being in the general vicinity he could not have avoided hearing the clamor from the brutal conflict between the goblins and the elves.

At the onset of the battle, Thrax had lumbered across the grasslands in the direction of the struggle evidently not appreciating the risk of being caught in the open, only pleased that he had found the elves at last. But the elves weren't his people any more than were the goblins that had stalked him for the past three days. Thrax crouched in the tall grass and considered what to do.

Clearly goblins aren't known for their loyalty under the best of circumstances. It took only a matter of moments for Thrax to resolve on a neutral stance, as either the elves or the goblin soldiers could be expected to kill him on sight. Noticing the hollowness of his belly, he concluded with admirable impartiality that it didn't really matter so much who won the fight as long as there was something left to eat in the end. That is where fate, in the form of a white horse, found him.

As it happened, in her rush to return to her mistress, Rosie very nearly ran Thrax down. I believe the mare may have actually charged him before recognizing him as the goblin she knew. She slid to a halt and stood before him with nostrils flaring. I don't know that Thrax believed in fate at that time; it's possible he never did, but he was young enough and reckless enough to recognize and take advantage of an opportunity. With an awkwardness unworthy of an elf, but an agility surprising for a goblin, Thrax climbed onto Rosie's back and off they went.

CHAPTER 18

*A*cross the grasslands Rosie raced, Thrax clinging to her neck as her mane whipped about his face. She broke through the first line of combatants without mishap, the elves and goblins so intent on their own diametrically opposed goals of continuing existence and extermination that they took little notice of the horse or her rider.

Then a stray arrow struck the back of a particularly massive goblin, a veritable gargantuan among goblins, and was deflected by his armor. He turned to see who fired the shot and unluckily saw the mare.

Howling savagely, the behemoth attacked, moving quickly despite his size and swinging an enormous mace. Rosie skidded, dodged and leapt into the air. For an instant she seemed to hang suspended, a shining, winged-Pegasus soaring over the goblin's head. But as remarkable as Rosie was, Rosie had no wings; she was an ordinary horse and could jump no higher than an ordinary horse could jump.

As she came down, the mace caught the tip of Rosie's left hind hoof, sending her tumbling. Landing on her shoulder, she somersaulted. Her rider sailed through the air sans horse, crashed into a tree trunk with a solid thud, and then slid to the ground and lay there in an untidy, unmoving heap.

Unhurt, Rosie bounded up and dodged through the trees searching for her mistress. Thrax staggered to his feet and followed, limping slightly.

Nolan had just slain the second of the three goblins that had breached the inner perimeter as Caedmon and Tomas battled the third, when Rosie burst into the clearing with Thrax on her heels. Catching movement from the corner of his eye, the prince spun nimbly around, bringing his sword to bear. Thrax deemed it appropriate to bare his fangs and snarl. Nolan, the prince, sworn protector of his people, raised his blade.

"Thrax! It's Thrax!" Finn cried out from his perch in the oak, as he almost fell from the tree in his haste to greet his friend. Scrambling to the ground, he rushed forward and clasped Thrax warmly around the knee. The snarl froze, and then slowly slipped from Thrax's face, replaced by an expression of such pained self-consciousness, such mortified chagrin, that Nolan had to laugh.

"So, this is Thrax." Nolan smiled as he shook his head in wonder, lowering his guard only slightly and not lowering his sword in the least.

"Kill him!" Tomas shouted, a bit ungraciously I thought. He and Caedmon had succeeded in slaying the last of the three goblins and were hurrying to join the prince.

It took a great deal of assurance on the part of Finn, and the more reluctantly offered endorsement of Kira to counter Tomas's insistence that Thrax must have been responsible for leading the other goblins in the attack on the camp. The evidence that Thrax had rescued Finn and protected Finn was undeniable; though Tomas refused to concede his belief that Thrax's motives for doing so could not have been anything approximating pure.

Thrax did nothing to advance his innocence in the assault on the elves; he merely stood by with a wickedly perverse expression on his face. As you may know, goblins like to take credit for any amount of mischief whether they actually have a hand in it or not. Still, in the end, his life was spared and Thrax was once again welcomed, more and less, into the community of the elves.

CHAPTER 19

*T*hough their attackers were vanquished, several members of the search party were killed and many were badly wounded. The gaiety of the morning was forgotten as the somber elves prepared to transport their dead and dying back to Surreydale. It was late in the day when the elves broke camp, but Nolan wisely chose to put as much distance as possible between his dispirited group and the scavengers that would gather in the dusk, drawn by the decaying flesh of the slain goblins.

The moon was full and the elves traveled into the night, stealing like wraiths through the shadows of the trees and only venturing into the open grasslands when no other path could be found. They were ill equipped for another run in with the goblins and so invoked all of their skills in remaining hidden while covering as much ground as possible in their forced march home. The prince's soldiers rode the few horses that were recovered, standing guard over the townsfolk and injured who traveled by foot or were carried. Tomas generously offered Rosie to the prince for his own use, but Nolan chose instead to walk with his people and assist in the transport of the wounded.

The journey home was as uneventful as could have been hoped for, though it of course took several days. Amias and Clare and many from the other search parties, not knowing of the battle but eager to celebrate the rescue of Finn, met Nolan's company when halfway to the bridge and assisted with the care of the injured.

Once the surviving elves had safely returned to Surreydale, a memorial service was held there to commemorate the slain. The townsfolk embraced Finn with enthusiasm and Thrax with reservation; though some felt Thrax's efforts to save Finn from the river were admirable, others simply could not overcome their deep-seated prejudices against him. Tomas was chief among the latter, though I thought I could perceive a slight softening in his attitude toward Thrax, a minimal thawing perhaps, brought on by his thankfulness that his grandson was alive and home.

CHAPTER 20

*T*hrax remained with the Strong family through the summer. I believe he was as happy as his nature would allow. Clare felt more gratitude than even her great heart could express, believing fully in Finn's story that Thrax had saved him and thanking the Great Creator daily for bringing Thrax into their lives. She embraced him as her own child, defended him against any unjust criticism and attempted to instill in him a pride in his own heritage, although actually most elves knew very little that was true about the origins of the goblins at that time.

The bond between Finn and Thrax grew, and they played together all summer: both traditional Elven games and games of their own creation and imagination. Thrax now seemed truly interested, if not invested, in the elves and their activities, as evidenced by his actions one morning in late July. It was a hot, dusty day. Kira had finished practicing her swordsmanship with one of her school chums and was fencing with her shadow when Thrax approached her.

"I should like to learn that, please. Would you be kind enough to teach me?"

Kira stopped and stared. It was the first time Thrax had initiated any conversation with her since he had come to stay with them. She could not have known that he had been practicing his short speech for weeks. He sounded just like an elf, like her father at the dinner table. "I should like a biscuit, please. Would you be kind enough to pass one 'round?"

Child that she was, Kira knew her mother and grandfather seriously disagreed about Thrax and his place in their family, though she didn't quite grasp the basis for it. She understood that her grandfather hated goblins, but Thrax wasn't just any goblin. Thrax was "their goblin" and had proven his worth by rescuing Finn. Still, she instinctively knew that her grandfather would very much disapprove of giving Thrax a sword. Being a child, she lacked the foresight to evaluate the potentially devastating consequences of teaching a goblin how to use one.

You see, at that time it was quite uncommon for a goblin to use a weapon that required skill to wield. Craftsmen were rare in their fluid communities and those that there were shaped objects suitable for a nomadic life: baskets, clay pots and water skins. Lacking any opportunities for instruction in the art of swordsmanship, a goblin that happened to pick up a sword as part of his plunder would tend to use it as a bat. Though the goblins that attacked the search party had pikes and poleaxes and were obviously expert in their deployment, your typical goblin used weapons of convenience: sticks, stones and bludgeons. Of course, a goblin's most formidable weapons have always been and likely always will be his claws and his teeth.

In spite of her vague uneasiness, Kira couldn't resist the opportunity for showing off her own skill in an activity in which she excelled. Lessons were undertaken and I had the opportunity of observing an amusing interaction that occurred later that same week.

Thrax and Kira were fencing. Kira advanced. Unused to the interplay of advancing and retreating, Thrax held his position until Kira was too close and then stumbled backward. Kira giggled as he hit the ground.

"You'll never be expert with a sword until you learn to stop tripping over your great big goblin feet!" she scolded as she stepped forward confidently, holding out her hand to help him up.

"Kill her!" Thrax told himself furiously. "How dare she laugh? How dare she!" He avoided her eyes so she wouldn't see her impending death and run.

"Don't be mad." Kira smiled down at him, though it was hardly down. He was almost as tall sitting as she was standing. "I was only teasing. It was a joke. You are expected to make a joke back."

Thrax looked up, still glowering.

"I'm going to take her hand and smack her so hard that her head will pop off and fly across the field," he thought.

According to goblin tenets such action would be condoned, even encouraged. So why did he hesitate?

Kira dropped her hand to her side.

"I'm sorry," she said, her forehead wrinkling as she tried to explain. "You don't understand. You're supposed to say something back. Like, "How'd you get those pointy ears? Did your Mom hang you from a clothesline when you were born?" Or else, say, "You should talk. You ride like a goblin," though I suppose that could reflect badly on us both."

Something funny was happening to his face. Thrax was fighting hard to maintain his scowl, but for some reason it was becoming difficult. As he looked away again, Kira bent down and took his hand. Her touch affected him in a queer way and he stood up very quickly. He snatched his hand away and wiped it on his pants, then stepped forward and backward a few times with his mouth hanging open.

"Our cultures must be very different," Kira said brightly, sounding somewhat precocious. "I didn't mean to offend you."

Thrax wiped his hand on his pants again. Finally, deciding his only means of preserving his dignity was to make a hasty retreat, he turned and walked quickly toward the house without saying a word, leaving his sword lying in the dirt.

Kira stood puzzling the matter over, but only for a moment, and then, picking up the sword, she laughed and ran off to the barn to find her brother.

I laughed too as I watched her go, enjoying the fleeting remembrance of youth; but then, I noticed that the wind had changed and turned back to my work in the garden.

CHAPTER 21

*F*rom the time of Finn's rescue, Prince Nolan and his soldiers scouted far and wide for the goblin army, but found no trace. They returned to the scene of the attack on the search party and carefully covered the area in all directions, but not a single goblin did they see, not even one of the usual kind. It was as if all goblins had vanished from the Wide World, but I of course knew they had not really gone.

I was away on business of my own when the attack on Surreydale occurred, though had I been near even I might not have been able to prevent the slaughter. It was September again, late in the afternoon, dusk but not yet dark. There was a chill in the air, a forewarning of an early frost.

Amias and Tomas were mending the corral fence near the southeast corner of the house. Kira and Finn were tending the horses and Clare, well, Clare was preparing stew while Thrax set the table for dinner.

Clare's child was due at any time and her increasing girth made working in the kitchen a challenge, though she still managed to carry herself with grace. Somehow Thrax had become her helpmate, a role that afforded the dual benefits of distracting Thrax from any real mischief and keeping him at an acceptable distance from Tomas. Thrax was tall enough to reach even the top shelves of the cabinets with ease, and I must say that being allowed to sample food as it was prepared had significantly improved his manners at the table.

Clare had her back to the window, stirring the pot, when Thrax glanced up to see Amias and Tomas battling at least 20 goblins in the front yard. Somehow they had crept quietly from the woods and attacked without warning. The goblins were dressed in armor and carried battleaxes and pikes.

The sound of plates crashing to the floor startled Clare and she turned in time to see Amias fall, stricken, clutching his neck as blood poured through his fingers. Tomas, bleeding badly from a wound to the leg, tumbled over backward in the wake of the onslaught, as the goblins ignored the old elf in their rush for the house.

Acting quickly because the occasion demanded it, Thrax rushed to bar the front door, and then hurried Clare toward the back as the invaders scrambled onto the porch. She stumbled in her haste and almost fell, catching hold of a stool to steady herself while her left hand went protectively to her belly.

Clare stood there for a long moment, very beautiful, very still, her hand on her abdomen, as if mesmerized, oblivious to the goblins crashing against the door. Then she looked up at Thrax and their eyes locked. One word escaped her pale lips.

"Please," she whispered, as her eyes filled with tears, and Thrax thought he knew what she meant. He shook his head.

"Please."

Reluctantly Thrax nodded.

Turning from her, he crossed to the hearth. Taking a sword from the display case above the mantel, he held it carefully as Kira had taught him. On your guard. As he gazed into her sky blue eyes, Thrax thrust the sharp blade straight through Clare's heart. She gasped once, but softly, and slumped forward, pinned by the blade.

Thrax stared as if in a dream, then pulled the sword back, letting Clare drop to the floor in a heap. Quickly he slashed twice across her great belly. He thought he saw something, like a tiny hand, protruding from the gaping wound, and then he turned away.

Through the window he glimpsed a quick movement at the barn door. Dashing out the back as the raiders burst through the front, Thrax flew across the yard. Kira and Finn met him at the door.

"Get back!" he said fiercely, shoving them roughly into the darkness of the hallway. Many of the horses were in the South pasture, but the few inside the barn were running wild in terror, crashing into the walls of their stalls. All except the old mare, Rosie. She stood quietly at her stall door, ears flicked forward.

"What's happening?" cried Kira, pulling Finn behind her to shield him with her own body.

"The goblins are here! You have to run!"

"My mother? My father?" Kira stared wide-eyed at the bloody sword in his hand.

"I'll do what I can for them!" His voice shook. "Now go!"

Thrax opened the door to the mare's stall and Rosie stepped out. Kira jumped, unassisted, to her back. Thrax lifted Finn up behind her.

"Ride to the village as fast as you can! Don't come back here! Don't ever come back!"

Thrax opened the other stall doors and the horses swept out. Rosie leapt into their midst. The barn door burst open and the raiders running across the yard from the house thought they saw Thrax leaping aside to avoid the rush of hooves. He feigned a grab at the trailing colt, but fell short as the other goblins howled in rage.

"I saw them escaping to the barn, but was too late to catch them," Thrax gasped, rising from the dusty earth. "I tried to hold the woman in the house for you, but she threw herself at me and I could not avoid killing her."

"Not as fresh. Not as fresh as could be, but still good," croaked one of the raiders, wiping his face with the back of his hand. "None left for you though, I'm afraid," he chuckled.

"There's the old elf in the front yard. Might be stringy, but I thinks he's not quite dead, yet," another croaked. He would not have offered except he was feeling quite full.

Thrax felt strangely numb, but was careful to hide it from the others. He followed, as if in a dream, around to the front of the house to look for Tomas. Amias lay bloody and still where he had fallen, his body desecrated beyond recognition, but Tomas was nowhere to be found.

"Where can he be? Where can he be?" asked one of the raiders, and a small wave of concern rippled through the group.

As if in answer, the bell in the watchtower began to ring loudly across the land. In the next moment, the sound of hunting horns filled the air followed closely by the clatter of hooves. The goblins scattered in all directions, making for the safety of the forest. Thrax stood as if undecided for just an instant, and then he was running, too.

"They'll kill me now for sure!" he told himself as he ran. "They'd never believe it wasn't me this time! They'll kill me now for sure."

CHAPTER 22

Many elves died in Surreydale that day, as the goblins attacked several of the farmhouses on the edge of Drae Woods. Jacob Turngood, whose leg had healed after his injury the previous fall, managed to use a pitchfork to fend off the goblins that cornered him in his barn loft, but both of his stout sons were caught in the fields and killed. His daughter Molly was luckily in town, and so escaped the slaughter.

Tomas survived his injuries and assumed the role of sole parent to Kira and Finn. Though he loved the children dearly, his bitterness occasionally spilled over into cold cruelty.

The massacre galvanized the elves as nothing else could do. No longer were there rumors of war; by this blatant, unprovoked attack on civilians, war had been waged. King Erron Thornehart declared a state of emergency and reluctantly invoked military rule. Prince Nolan helped organize a militia to patrol and protect the more isolated communities within his realm.

Due to his skill at the forge, Tomas was invited to live at Heath Downs where he provided oversight for the manufacture of swords and supplied horses for the soldiers. Though it broke the hearts of Kira and Finn, the remarkable Strong family horses were pressed into service as the elves assembled an army.

And what of Thrax? Let's just say that any influence Clare might have had over him for good vanished in the instant she died. Thrax became the most fearsome, most vicious goblin of his time. His acts of savagery were legend, beginning the very evening of the day he left Surreydale.

CHAPTER 23

*T*hrax was then eleven years old. As he fled from the town and the elves and the only home he'd ever known, he found himself keeping pace with several of the goblins from the battle, if you could call it such. At first he ran blindly, so shocked by the unexpected turn of events that reason evaded him and comprehension was impossible; but as night fell, shards of the grisly happenings of the day began to pierce his protective shell of insentience, driving his feelings to expression.

The goblins were loping along in cadence, covering ground quickly, their soft footfalls not unlike the sound of a beating heart. Thrax had kept the sword from the mantel case and it occurred to him to notice that some of Clare's blood had run from the tip down the blade and onto his hand. The thought horrified him and he had to resist the urge to fling the sword away.

Bits of conversation began to seep into his consciousness, words spoken by the other goblins as they hurried south through the woods.

"We showed them elves; we did."

"Just like He said…"

"Always thinkin' they's better than us."

"Tasty they was; specially her…"

Thrax frowned, blinked and swallowed. Reflexively, he tightened his grip on the sword.

"He says we'll have all we wants."

"Specially her..."

Howling in anguish and unspeakable rage, Thrax struck with such ferocity and force that one stroke sent the speaker's head spinning through the air where it bounced from tree to tree until it disappeared into the darkness. The other goblins slowed, puzzled, not fully grasping what had happened or the significance of it.

These were six fully-grown goblins. All had survived many battles and killed many times, yet they quailed when they saw the queer light in Thrax's eyes. Of the six, only one lived long enough to tell the tale, his story whispered to those who found him moments before he joined his companions in death. He spoke the truth of what happened, accompanied by dire warnings, though few believed him at the time. The goblins fought savagely, until fierceness gave way to fear and flight. They fought skillfully, with pikes and axes and claw and tooth. Still one half-grown goblin with a sword overcame them, slashed and maimed them and left them all for dead.

Time passed and the world changed. For fifteen years, the elves and the goblins waged war continuously but on a small scale, neither side clearly victorious or vanquished. Though the goblin army might have more easily annihilated the elves, Maelstrom's goal of dominating them was proving elusive.

Thrax's reputation as a cold killer grew and spread throughout the Eastern realms and into the South as well. He murdered indiscriminately, without conscience or thought, goblins, elves, men. As he matured in size and strength, he progressed from the sword to a short knife as his weapon of choice; Thrax reveled in the horror he could generate slipping through shadowy places stalking his prey, but he preferred to be close for the kill.

Thrax became the cautionary tale told to ill-mannered children aimed to induce improvements in bad behavior. Thrax was the story whispered by grown men around the campfire at night that made them laugh merrily as they sat together, but robbed them of sleep once they were alone.

Thrax was everywhere and nowhere for fifteen years, often spoken of but seldom seen, only glimpsed in brief moments of terror by those whose lives he took. Then one afternoon I was out of my usual way, passing through Crompton, when I chanced to catch sight of him going into the Owl's Eye Tavern. I should not have recognized him except for the scar on his arm, which had been enhanced by ink in shades of black and red to resemble the shape of a great hideous serpent. Curiosity overcame me and I followed him in.

CHAPTER 24

*T*he busy, bustling, raucous room fell silent when Thrax entered, but then became noisy again as the majority of the patrons seemed to remember they had other places to be. Chairs slid back, coins clinked on tables and the scuffle of boots marked a mass exodus to the door.

Two goblins remained at the sagging bar, alone, as the barkeep discreetly stepped away. One was aged, edentulous and unkempt, with wispy tufts of grey hair sprouting from his pate, the typical nomadic goblin in later life. The other was unlike any goblin I had seen. Slender he was and fair, with golden skin and a thick head of fiery red hair. His tawny eyes were in stark contrast to the other's dark green ones. He was near Thrax's age, perhaps even a summer or two younger, and he carried himself with an imperial air that would have set him apart even in the absence of his obvious physical distinctiveness. The golden goblin stood as Thrax approached.

"You must be Thrax," he said politely. "I am Josef."

He bowed slightly, a universal sign of greeting and re-spect.

"And this is Scred." He indicated his companion, who bowed also, albeit shakily and without looking up.

Thrax did not return the greeting, but instead slouched carelessly onto one of the rough-hewn stools. I was struck by the changes time and circumstance had wrought. Gone was the lanky, clumsy youth that had skulked in the hedges watching the Elven children at play. In his place was a hideous, hulking predator. His every movement seemed controlled and calculated to intimidate.

"You wanted to see me?" he growled. His voice was harsh and hollow, like brittle bones baked white by the sun.

"I did," answered Josef, sitting back down, "and I thank you for coming, but where is my messenger, Tormey?"

"He happened along as I was just thinking of lunch." Thrax smiled coldly. "Luckily he didn't die so quick that he couldn't tell me of your...interest."

Josef looked surprised and displeased. Scred made a sound in his throat, something between a snort and a whimper, before quaffing down his ale.

"That was unnecessary," Josef began sternly, a rebuke he left unfinished when Thrax turned to face him.

For a moment they were silent as each took the other's measure. I had the impression that Thrax was challenging Josef only to see how he would respond; though I was also quite sure Tormey was dead. Josef must have realized it was all a part of the game. He recalled his directive and continued smoothly.

"...but not relevant to the matter at hand. Our Lord Maelstrom would like to present you with an opportunity to serve your people. He believes that your unique skills make you particularly qualified for this purpose."

Thrax picked his teeth with a long, filthy fingernail.

"What's in it for me?"

"The gratitude of Lord Maelstrom and the satisfaction of knowing you have served your fellow goblins in a worthy cause," Josef replied promptly. His manner bordered on condescension, but Thrax did not seem to notice or care.

"Yeah? What's that worth?"

Josef frowned and took a small sip of ale, his expression of disdain now approaching disgust. The liquid was cloudy, obviously not to his satisfaction, and he swirled the dregs in his glass.

"There may be a financial component to Lord Maelstrom's gratitude," he offered carefully.

Thrax smirked and scratched his chin.

"We may have something to discuss then. What's the "opportunity"?"

As I listened, it occurred to me suddenly that neither Thrax nor Josef was conversing in what I had always considered as the normal goblin dialect. Josef's speech patterns were pedantic, reminding me of the Highborough elves, and Thrax was adapting his responses accordingly based on his experiences with the elves in Surreydale. Josef seemed to observe this as well and was pleased by it.

"I believe Lord Maelstrom is correct in his opinion of you," Josef said, his disapproval giving way to grudging endorsement. "You may actually be perfect for this assignment."

"And again, what is the "assignment"?"

"Espionage," answered Josef, causing Thrax to sit up a little straighter.

"Espionage?" Thrax's green eyes glowed as he tested the word. He liked the sound of it.

"Espionage."

As Josef explained, I at first thought his plan ludicrous. Judging by the expression on Thrax's face, he would not have disagreed. On the surface, it seemed quite impossible. Thrax was to pose as an elf and infiltrate the royal guard at Heath Downs. Once there he would gather tactical information and provide reports of the elves' forces, armaments, strengths and weaknesses to Lord Maelstrom through his contact, Josef. Based on Thrax's reports, the Goblin Lord would determine the most efficient method of overcoming the elves at Heath Downs as one step in his overall strategy for dominance in the goblin/elf wars.

"You do not believe this proposal is sensible," Josef stated, before Thrax could point out the marked improbability of success in such a venture.

"Scred, please show Thrax what you have in your pocket."

Scred swilled the last of his ale and glanced up hopefully, but the discreet barkeep had not returned. Sighing heavily, he rose and shuffled reluctantly forward.

Without taking his eyes from Josef, and for no reason that I could then determine, Thrax reached out suddenly and throttled the old goblin. Scred struggled and choked, but Josef simply raised his eyebrows. He voiced no remonstration, nor did he move to intervene on behalf of his companion. Scred's face turned red and then blue as his eyes bulged. Finally Josef spoke.

"If you kill Scred, he cannot show you what he has in his hand."

Thrax maintained his grip for a moment longer, and then nodded, apparently satisfied. He smiled and released Scred, who fell back coughing and trembling and gasping for breath.

"Show him please," said Josef.

"He doesn't wants it," Scred croaked, touching his neck tenderly with knobby fingers as he looked fearfully at Thrax.

"Show him," ordered Josef. Something in his tone forced the old goblin forward, though with even less enthusiasm than he had initially shown.

To his surprise, Thrax saw that Scred held a medallion, a small gold talisman, attached to a long, thin chain.

"What is it?" Thrax asked curiously, not taking his eyes from the glittering gold.

"'S magic!" Scred nodded, his wrinkled face splitting into an unexpected grin as he whispered conspiratorially, "'S for you!"

"For me?" Thrax frowned. "Get off!" He shoved the old goblin angrily.

"No, no. 'S magic for you!" Scred insisted, holding the fetish out toward Thrax.

"You think I'm going to wear that thing? A freaking necklace?" Thrax was rapidly losing his patience. "What do I look like to you?"

"You looks like a goblin, a great goblin, the most virilest of goblins," Scred assured Thrax solemnly. He reached out as if to pat Thrax encouragingly on his shoulder, but withdrew his hand quickly when he saw the look in Thrax's eyes. The old goblin swallowed hard to be sure he still could and then continued.

"But you puts this on and you don't looks like any kinds of goblins at all," Scred explained, a spark of something surprisingly shrewd reflected in his rummy eyes. "You puts this on and you looks like...an elf!"

CHAPTER 25

W hile Thrax had been evolving into all things that goblins admire and aspire to, our noble Prince Nolan had also felt the effects of time. The most obvious alteration, of course, was in his appearance, but there were other changes less apparent, at least at first glance. Prince Nolan's face though still youthful was now lined with care, and his dark hair was salted with grey, and there was a sadness bordering on despair that shone in his once confident eyes.

It was still spring, a crisp, bright day, only a few short weeks after my unexpected sighting of Thrax, when Prince Nolan reined in his mount and gazed southwest through the treetops of the Wuthering Wood. In the distance he could just make out the lofty spires of the House at Heath Downs. Located on the edge of The Carrick, the castle rose above the surrounding countryside creating a picturesque and tactically impenetrable vista.

The prince and his soldiers had been traveling for seven days and nights, journeying home from Loaghaire, the north-most outpost of King Thornehart's realm. Finn, now grown and a captain of the guard, rode at his prince's side. Though Nolan's trip had been successful in its stated purpose, his homecoming was bittersweet.

Three months he had spent in Loaghaire, fortifying the town's defenses and training all those who were able in the latest best practices against goblin invasion. Three months away from the House at Heath Downs: a self-imposed exile. He need not have gone; he might have sent Finn alone, but hoped his time away would provide some much-needed perspective. In a way, it had. Observing firsthand the toll the war was taking on his people had reinforced his grim determination to let nothing stand in the way of defeating the goblins at last.

"Let's stop here and rest for a moment in the shade." Now that Heath Downs was within sight, Nolan found himself unexpectedly reluctant to continue on.

Dismounting stiffly, he handed his reins to Cormac and turned to find Finn. A movement of no matter saved his life, for as he turned the iron-tipped pike that had been aimed at the center of his chest pierced his shoulder instead.

Drawing his sword, Cormac cried out as he leapt to the aid of his fallen prince, but his warning came too late. A dozen pikes sailed through the air, many finding their targets, and goblins appeared from the ether.

An ambush! The goblins had been waiting! But how had they crept so close to Heath Downs? How had they known the prince would be there in the woods?

Out-numbered two to one, the elves had no time to ponder the gross deficiencies responsible for this extraordinary failure in their security measures. Howling savagely, the goblins swarmed forward brandishing their maces and halberds. Those elves still standing drew swords and bows while scrambling to form a battle line between their attackers and their fallen friends.

"To me! To me!" Finn called, as he rallied his troops. Hearing their captain's voice, the soldiers spread out to form a rough circle around him, knowing that Prince Nolan would be somewhere near the center of the ring. Though trained in the use of weapons, the goblins were not shrewd enough to realize that the elves now had a tactical advantage: a common goal. They would die to protect their prince. Unfortunately, it looked as if their deaths would be meaningless; Prince Nolan lay pale and bleeding on the ground, the pike tip and its shaft extending in either direction from his wound.

The battle raged, more elves dying than goblins, as the defenders were overrun by the superior size and number of their foes. Holes opened rapidly in the elves' defensive line requiring a contraction of the circle around the prince. Initially Finn remained slightly within the perimeter, rushing forward quickly to block encroachments, buying time for the line to close again. As the elves fell, he moved to the line himself, fighting hand to hand with goblins more that three times his size.

Finn, though young, was extraordinarily skilled in combat and had attained his rank as captain through merit alone. The warrior Cathmor had taken an interest in him shortly after the tragic and brutal slaying of his parents, and the young elf had proven a worthy pupil. The old soldier lived still, but traveled rarely. Yet, whenever Finn was in battle the specter of Cathmor loomed at his back, almost seeming a tangible presence, whispering in Finn's ear, counseling him when to strike and when to retreat as Finn boldly faced Death for the sake of his kinsmen and king.

Of the twenty Elven soldiers that had entered the woods, only eight now stood between the goblins and the prince. Within sight of the castle, they might as well have been across The Endless Blue; the elves had no means of calling for reinforcements, no reason to expect help of any kind. That is why the sound of a hunting horn, close by and clear, caused both sides to pause in surprise. The goblins looked about anxiously, wondering if another company of soldiers had somehow happened upon the scene, but the horn fell silent and the butchery continued.

Then suddenly, impossibly, a ninth elf seemed to spring from the very earth to join the eight desperate defenders as they clashed with the goblins only a short length away from their fallen prince.

The stranger was tall and wore a ragged, brown cloak, but the sword he held flashed bright and true. With a few quick strokes, he beheaded one goblin and disemboweled another while the other elves watched in stunned appreciation. Disheartened before his arrival, the elves fought with renewed vigor as the newcomer led them in a counterattack, driving the goblins back into the trees.

The goblins yowled in dismay, as the strange elf seemed to be everywhere at once, cat-quick and deadly. No resistance they could offer slowed him and any injuries inflicted upon him only seemed to inspire him to further violence. The tide of war had turned and now the goblins were dying in droves. Many sought to escape into the woods, only to fall at the hand of the tall stranger. Finally all was silence and the elves stared wide-eyed at the carnage that remained.

Finn stepped forward as the stranger turned toward him. Like his mother, Finn was tall and fair, with hair the color of moonbeams and eyes like the sky. He would have been almost as handsome as Clare had been beautiful but for the jagged scar that marred his features, causing the skin to draw tightly across his left cheek.

"I am Finn Strong," he said, "captain of the guard, protector of Nolan Thornehart, Crown Prince of the Eastern Elves."

"Jac Savitch," the stranger replied, bowing, "at your service." He was taller even than Finn, with dark hair and darker eyes.

"I do not know the name, but you are obviously a warrior of some renown." The statement contained a question. Finn stood at ease but did not sheath his sword.

"I am probably best known in the Western realm, though since goblins took my family I have called no land my home. I've been a wanderer for these fifteen years and only chance brought me here to this place on this day. I had no idea your prince was in danger, only that elves were fighting goblins and when goblins are being killed I must have my share of the fun."

The stranger smiled sardonically at this last comment, and Finn studied his face thoughtfully.

"You have saved my prince and my life," he observed, and Thrax was astonished by the changes that had erased the 5-year-old boy he had known and replaced him with this 20-year-old soldier. "You must join our party and accompany us to Heath Downs."

Polite though this offer seemed, it had more the sound of an order than a request. Thrax touched the talisman at his neck and chuckled to himself. So far, all was going as planned.

CHAPTER 26

*A*fter bearers had rushed from the woods with the prince, and runners had been sent to bring medical assistance for the wounded, Finn went from elf to elf providing what care he could. Only when all his soldiers were attended and in route did he walk back with Thrax, posing as Jac Savitch, to introduce him to the Home Guard and find him a place to stay.

"Roaming the land for fifteen years, and have you no horse?" Finn asked curiously as they strode among the trees.

Sunlight, sifted through new leaves, created shifting patterns on the soft earth. A faint hint of cardamom scented the air. But for the ambush, the killing and the dying, it must have been a pleasant afternoon.

"Not at present," Thrax replied truthfully enough, and then added, "Without a permanent home, I haven't the means to keep one."

He spoke rather slowly, as if considering each word, but his intonation was flawless. Had I not possessed the gift of Sight, even I should not have known him for what he was.

The forest ended abruptly at the base of the escarpment and Thrax forgot himself entirely as he gazed up in amazement at Heath Downs: the stronghold of the Eastern Elves.

CHAPTER 27

*L*ong before the Eminent Wars, even before The Current Days, an ancient and advanced race built a massive citadel in the Carrick Mountains, high on a plateau, thirty feet above the forest floor. A marvel of engineering, the construction of such a bastion, tucked into and surrounded on three sides by sheer rock, was obviously the work of many lifetimes of toil.

The elves had come into ownership several hundred years past, but not by conquest. The peoples of the unknown civilization, for reasons unapparent, had abandoned or been driven from their mountain fortress centuries before the first elf crept up the ramp and through the massive gates of the outer wall. Though the elves by now knew many of the secrets of their adopted capital, still scholars from Highborough spent seasons studying the strange language and carvings inscribed by Heath Down's original inhabitants on crumbling monuments and plaques; these preserved with care by Elven historians.

Only one entrance to this formidable sanctuary could be seen from the forest. The enormous ramp that extended from the base of The Carrick, as the escarpment was called, to its plateau led through the gates of the barbican. Stone machicolations projected from the battlements of the outer wall and archers could be glimpsed in the arrow loops. Thrax, who was evaluating the fortress with an invader's eye, could only hope that there were additional paths of access to Heath Downs through the mountains, though the stark, razor-sharp peaks that loomed over the city did not appear either inviting or accessible.

As the two mounted the ramp, Thrax mentally noted the location and number of the sentries as Finn paused to comment on some of the natural wonders of the region. Their elevation afforded a striking view: the Eastern realm spread before them, a brilliant, jeweled tapestry.

North of Heath Downs, Loch L'Aurin slept deep in a mountain basin; liquid gold, her placid surface rarely disturbed by the least of breezes. Her temperate waters perpetually rippled down into Castalia Spring, which wound lazily along the base of The Carrick before emptying into and connecting Loch L'Aurin to her southern sister, Mirror Lake. Home to the mythical Muses, Castalia Spring was fabled to have healing powers and had, prior to the goblin/elf wars, attracted visitors from throughout the Wide World.

To the east, and barely visible beyond the trees, the mighty Rione shimmered like spun silver, tumbling from the ice-capped Suraelian Mountains, rushing past the quaking aspen and spruce of the Wuthering Wood, cutting through the very heart of the Eastern elves' territory. The Rione's channel ran deep near its origin, forming the shadowy Grosborn Gorge, and became wider further south as the valley broadened and the river sped past Surreydale and into Loch Donla.

Directly south were the grasslands, extending to the very rim of the world, a sea of rustling, faded yellow mixed with the jade green of new spring growth. As Finn continued his description of the topography, I wonder that Thrax was not reminded of his adventures in the Bluefield Marsh, but Thrax was listening to Finn with only one ear. His sole focus was his mission, or so it seemed.

The two wandered slowly through the portcullis, the heavy vertical gate of the inner wall, and into the city, pausing one final time to survey the countryside from the edge of the cliff face before turning from the bucolic to the urbane. The transition was abrupt, and for Thrax, who was accustomed to the pastoral, somewhat discordant; the primary note struck being a strong sense of a society at war.

Immediately within the inner wall and to the left of the gates was a stone gatehouse; four armed sentries stood watch at the door. Low wooden barracks lined the inner wall to the south and west. Beyond the barracks, Thrax could see storage buildings, and further in the distance, the stables.

A battalion of soldiers was assembled in The Quarter, preparing to ride out in search of any goblins left and living within the elves' realm. Other elves moved among the barracks, going about their assigned duties with purposeful strides. Thrax gazed about, trying quickly to sort a myriad of visual impressions into a concise and orderly form. His distraction, at an inopportune moment, led to immediate mishap.

"Liam!" Finn called, putting his hand on Thrax's shoulder to steer him toward a nearby group of elves.

Goblins, as you would expect, are not accustomed to being touched, especially in a sociable way.

Before he could think to stop himself, Thrax raised his arm and shoved his elbow backward, aiming a disabling, if not potentially fatal, blow at his startled companion's throat. Though not anticipating an attack of this sort, Finn was not unprepared. The agile elf nimbly ducked, grabbing Thrax's arm with both hands and stepping behind him, letting Thrax's own weight and momentum carry him to the earth.

All were stunned, but none more than Thrax; no one had thrown him in fifteen years. Several nearby elves, hearing the commotion without knowing the cause, rushed forward with swords unsheathed. The gatehouse sentries stood suspended in disbelief, laughing in surprise more than actual glee. Thrax started up, his eyes glowing green, his anger immediate and palpable.

"Are you all right?" Finn asked politely, no trace of amusement in his voice or manner. He reached out his hand to assist his fallen comrade as if nothing out of the usual had happened.

I must admit I was astonished by how quickly Thrax regained his composure. He had apparently made substantial progress in learning to control his impulsive goblin nature. He shook his head with the appearance of amiability, gripped Finn's hand firmly and scrambled to his feet. Then he chuckled mirthlessly.

"You are obviously a warrior of some renown as well," he said, bowing as he spoke. "And I have been living in the wilderness without the company of my fellow elves for far too long. I expect only enemies even when surrounded by friends."

I thought I detected a grudging note of respect in his voice.

"We all become what circumstance requires," Finn replied shortly, and then turned to the elf that had joined them.

"Liam," he said, "this is Jac Savitch, a champion from the West. Jac has done us a great service today and needs a place to stay. Liam Anders is sergeant of the Home Guard."

Liam bowed at the introduction. "I will see to it."

Tall and thin, Liam Anders had a waif-like appearance that was incongruous with the weapons he carried. Though his manner was brisk and soldierly, his pale eyes spoke a dreamers' haziness that hinted at distraction; a gentle mind at odds with the present, lost somewhere in the future or the past.

Liam politely gestured for Thrax to precede him, indicating the nearest set of barracks to his left.

"But first," he offered, "would you care for something to eat?"

Thrax nodded his approval. "Yes, something to eat."

As he dusted off his pants, he discreetly and covetously eyed the brace of knives strapped to Liam's right thigh and pondered the possible purpose for the metal disks fixed to his belt.

"I must speak with the King," Finn remarked as he turned to go. He paused. "But, I will return later this afternoon. I would like to show you around the city."

"Thank you," Thrax replied, ever so appropriately, though certainly without sincerity. "I should appreciate that very much.

CHAPTER 28

W hile Thrax feigned enjoyment of military rations and Finn hurried through the city alone, bearers carried Prince Nolan quickly down the great hall of the castle keep. On the walls he could see the portraits of previous Elven rulers, once fearless and strong, now dead and dust, their regal faces turned toward him in vague apprehension as he passed.

The pike's shaft had been broken off, and the prince's bleeding assuaged. For fear of causing additional harm, the pike's tip was left in his shoulder for the surgeon to remove. Prince Nolan's face was drawn and his breathing shallow. He closed his eyes to conceal his pain from those who transported him, not wishing to add to the concern he knew they must already feel.

The sound of running footsteps echoed through the hall and the prince opened his eyes. In a moment, Kira was beside him.

"My Prince," her voice broke as she gazed upon his pale face, "I came as soon as I heard."

"There is no need to worry, My Lady," he whispered. "All will be well."

Prince Nolan's attempt to speak normally met with limited success. His words came out in short gasps, causing his companion's expression to darken further.

"I am a selfish creature, as you know, and I cannot bear to lose you," she cried. " You and Finn are the only family I have left! You must be well. Don't forget that you promised to serve in my father's place when Devin and I wed."

"You are now and ever will be my family," Nolan replied with a wan smile. "You needn't marry my brother to make it so."

Kira smiled and clutched his hand tightly as she hurried down the hall by his side. I don't believe she realized the true import of Nolan's words, or the nature of his regard for her, and so she wounded him further.

"You tease me, but I am quite in earnest. There can be no wedding without you."

"We must take him in to the surgeon, My Lady," interrupted Wim, as they reached the broad mahogany doors.

"It will be fine, Kira," assured Nolan. "Now go and find Finn."

Her smile held until the doors closed, and then tears filled her eyes and her shoulders shook with silent weeping.

CHAPTER 29

*T*hrax had never in his life seen anything like the House at Heath Downs. He wondered why it was even called a "house" as it bore no resemblance to the simple, single-story structures most elves called home. The House at Heath Downs was a castle, a palace, a dwelling place of kings for time out of mind.

True to his word, Finn returned to escort Thrax around the city and even a goblin could not help but be favorably impressed by the organizational skills and ingenuity of the elves.

Under direction of the Council for War, gardens and livestock were kept and maintained in the northern section of the city, providing provisions to withstand a siege of many months' duration. Supplies and equipment were housed in the southern section. Through the middle, a myriad of quaint shops and markets gave way to the library and other public buildings that lined the paved walk to the House. A circular wall of stone and the House Guard separated the palace and its denizens from the residential areas of the community.

As they strolled amongst the flower stands and stalls, Thrax engaged in his version of polite conversation, though Finn likely thought him remarkably course. You must recall that Thrax had become a killer for sport and gain, an occupation that favored the taciturn and solitary. His alter ego, Jac Savitch, in contrast was quite verbose, almost overbearingly so. Perhaps Thrax in his eagerness to support the charade of being an elf strayed on the side of too much disclosure. Espionage was, after all, a new venue for him.

The day was waning as the two crossed the courtyard and approached the castle. The sun had fallen below the mountain peaks, leaving the House in early dusk.

"Might I possibly check in on your prince?" Thrax asked, with deference, and I'm sure no real regard for Nolan.

"We can request a report on his condition," Finn agreed. He nodded to the guard as he led Thrax through the archway. Two sentries armed with halberds moved to open the heavy doors.

The floor of the front hall was polished marble-black laced with red-and the wall panels were mahogany, stained dark and rich with age. The ceiling was high and covered with bright lamps that chased the evening's shadows into far corners, but Thrax's attention was immediately drawn to a figure, the only inhabitant of the room.

She was standing with her back to him, looking out the tower window. Thrax felt an odd sensation in his chest and knew instinctively that it was Kira. She turned and smiled brightly. The eight-year-old child in pigtails had become a young lady. Small and dark, Thrax could see none of Clare in her.

"My sister, Kira Strong," said Finn, by way of introduction. "Kira, this is the warrior we spoke of earlier."

"It is a pleasure to meet you, Jac Savitch. You have saved many lives today!" she exclaimed, extending her hand.

Thrax hesitated, but imperceptibly so, and then stepped boldly forward and took her hand, bowing from the waist.

"My Lady," he said softly, "it was nothing." And he laughed to himself because he knew it really was.

CHAPTER 30

*A*nd so, once again Thrax came to live among the elves. Maelstrom's plan, as fantastic as it had originally sounded, was meeting with unequivocal success. Thrax in his guise as Jac Savitch moved freely about Heath Downs, conversing with the soldiers and even with members of the royal household. His request to be housed in the barracks was not acquiesced to by Finn, who insisted Jac have his own small private room outside the guardhouse, but no one seemed concerned if he chose to watch training exercises or had questions about the elves' strategies for defense.

One thing Thrax noticed immediately was this: though in farming communities male and female elves assumed what were considered traditional roles, the husband working the fields while his wife maintained the household, in times of war, gender was irrelevant. The elves have always differed from the other so-called advanced races in this respect. Female elves were integral to the Elven army and though most were trained in the use of lighter weapons, the bow and sometimes the sword, they fought along side their male counterparts with equal fierceness and determination.

While Finn's position as captain of the guard was unanticipated and therefore of interest, Kira's as a sword master was inconceivable to Thrax. Little Kira teaching elves to kill? How could that be? Though not a philosopher by any estimation, even Thrax could not help seeing how much the elves had lost and how ill suited they were as a race to carry on a war.

"How," he wondered, "have they managed to avoid enslavement?"

Maelstrom was expecting Thrax to provide the answer to this question and Thrax was uniquely placed to do so. His greatest difficulty now was in getting in and out of the city to pass any information he gleaned along to Josef.

You see, though the elves had welcomed Thrax, or Jac Savitch as they knew him, into their homes, Thrax was confident, and correctly so, that he was being watched; perhaps not followed, but certainly watched. He had stalked enough victims to know. Josef had instructed Thrax on a time and place for their first meeting, but had offered no suggestions whatever for keeping their rendezvous without creating suspicion, leaving Thrax solely to his own devices.

He did not imagine the elves could be so very gullible as to trust him, a stranger, to wander in and out of their city at will, or could they? Thrax remembered how Amias and Clare had saved his life and how he had planned to repay them by killing them in their sleep. Then, there was the wolf.

Kira had found him as a cub, attacked by his own kind and dying in the woods near Castalia Spring. Kira, who had almost lost her life to the wolves in Drae Woods the night Finn had fallen into the river, took the pup in and, in spite of opposition from her friends and family, nursed it back to health. Though the wolf was now healthy and grown, still it stayed at Heath Downs, following Kira around as if she were its mother.

But, was the wolf the playful pet and protector it seemed, or was it something else? Thrax had his reasons to wonder.

The wolf had taken an undue interest in him, showing more curiosity about Thrax than it had done for anyone before according to Kira. The elves may not have followed Thrax, but the wolf did, and frequently. Several times each day, Thrax caught a glimpse of the wolf's shadow as it slipped through hedges and shrubs, keeping pace with him as he scouted the city. After a time Thrax came to suspect that the wolf had somehow sensed what he really was, yet it didn't raise an alarm.

Amias and Clare had taken Thrax in and Kira had done the same for the wolf. Perhaps, he thought, the elves were just that foolish; but if so, how had they survived as long as they had? How had they managed to fend off Maelstrom's army for the past fifteen years? Thrax was determined to know.

CHAPTER 31

*T*hrax had been living in Heath Downs for the better part of two weeks before he stumbled on a means for leaving the city unattended; I'm sure to him it seemed an eternity. By that time, he had come very close to killing several of the elves.

You see, Thrax was accustomed to hunting whenever he chose and practiced his vocation with cheerful and compulsive regularity. Confined as he was with innumerable potential victims, the lust for blood was growing, nearing uncontrollable, when chance intervened and proffered a solution, an opportunity he all but missed, disguised as it was as misfortune that could have just as easily led to his downfall.

The original developers of Heath Downs had designed a complex arrangement of cisterns to collect and store the rainwater that flowed down the Carrick Mountains for both household use and separately for irrigation. The elves, adapting the system for their own way of life, added elf-made channels throughout the city designated for recreational purposes.

It was the brink of summer, and the water had only recently warmed to a degree that was tolerable for leisure use. Thrax stood unseen as Kira walked quietly down to the river that ran behind the palace park. He was familiar by now with the habits of the household and knew she went

for a swim almost every morning. It seemed of no conse-
quence to him that he was in the same vicinity on most
days.

"Just a coincidence," he told himself, but I suspect it
was something else. He noticed that the wolf was with her,
and then saw it lay down on the bank a few feet away.

"So is he tame," Thrax wondered, "or, not?"

He heard a splash and moved to a better vantage point
so that he could see Kira in the water. She swam like a fish,
lithe and graceful.

"She doesn't even know I'm here," he thought with
pride, "in spite of my goblin feet."

And Thrax felt some of the resentment he had felt as a
child.

"But," he reflected, "she actually did me a huge favor,
though she didn't know it. She trained me so that I could
spy on her and her brother and all their stupid people."

He smiled to himself in satisfaction and felt the resentment fade.

"Yes, she did me a favor. I will have to thank her for
that, after I show her exactly who I really am, right before
she dies."

Thrax was startled from his reverie by a slight movement on the opposite side of the river. He caught the
motion out of the corner of his eye, and turned to look.

"What was that?"

Something large and reptilian had slipped into the water without making a sound and he could see a very small wake as the strange beast moved effortlessly through the current toward Kira. Kira hadn't seen it, but Thrax noticed the wolf watching the shape as it moved closer.

"So, you are not tame," Thrax thought.

The wolf was making no effort to alert Kira to the danger.

"She's still a fool, trusting and blind." He snorted in disgust.

It made Thrax angry that Kira had learned so little from the death of her parents.

"Guess she'll die a little sooner than planned. It's a wonder she lasted this long. Her brother will be crushed, of course. Sad for him, but good for me."

He watched the creature as he mused on the possible advantages of Kira's imminent death. As I mentioned, he was no philosopher, but was learning strategy from playing war games with Finn.

"Guess she's not going to notice it until it bites her," Thrax snorted again, and rolled his eyes. "Where's all that elf sixth sense stuff? Guess her pointed ears don't work so good…"

He had been leaning against a tree, but now he stood straighter, fascinated as the creature moved to within a few yards of Kira.

Kira stopped swimming and looked around, alert now, treading water. Thrax crept forward.

"She knows it's there, finally!" he thought, exasperated. "Let's see how well she dies."

In the next second, the beast surged forward and Kira dove deep. She was down a long time and came up half way to the bank. To Thrax's surprise, she didn't scream.

"Why doesn't she call out?" he wondered. "Why doesn't she call for help?"

The Home Guard was certainly within earshot and would rush to her aid.

Then he saw her eyes, wide open and sky blue, sky blue, just like Clare's. Quicker than thought, Thrax was moving though the trees and toward the river. Kira had gone under again and came up several yards upstream and closer to the bank, but not close enough. The creature no longer wasted time in stealth and set the water boiling as it rushed after her.

Twenty feet from the edge of the river, Thrax leapt from an outcropping of rocks and flung himself straight into the water. No hesitation, no emotion, no plan. He was, before all things, a killer and something was about to die.

The creature turned to meet him in the water. It was at least thirty feet from tip to tail. Jaws wide, razor sharp teeth gleaming, its cold eyes closed as it rolled sideways to strike. Thrax lunged backward to avoid the charge, but too slowly, and he felt the palms of his hands rip on the scaly hide as he grappled for a hold. The taste of blood drove the creature to madness and it circled quickly to strike again.

Kira had almost made it to land and the wolf, realizing that her rescue was inevitable, sounded the alarm with a series of short barks. She called out to the guards, who hastened to join her, drawing their arrows and fitting them to their bows as they ran.

Water, scales and blood spewed into the air as the combatants collided with fracturing force. Thrax wrapped his great arms around the monster's snout, and, ignoring the tearing of his own flesh, shoved its head up and back in an attempt to break its spine. The force of his attack flipped the creature's body into the air and then submerged them both. Time was suspended and Kira held her breath for her rescuer as seconds turned to minutes. The river was still. The archers waited anxiously with bows taunt for any sign of beast or elf.

Then, with a roar and a splash, the opponents erupted from the water, so tightly entwined that the archers had no clear target without putting their own at risk. Thrax was bleeding profusely from a gash above his eye, horrifying to the spectators even from a distance; still he scarcely blinked so intent was he on the battle.

Flipping its enormous tail, the beast began to roll; those on the bank cried out in warning and Thrax gasped for breath before he was plunged down into the murky deep. Flashes of bright scale mixed with gore churned in the water around him as Thrax fumbled for the short blade at his belt. The creature's hide was thick, but not impenetrable.

Up they came again, the beast roaring in pain, defiance and fear as Thrax buried his knife to the hilt in its chest. Twisting violently, the beast wrenched free and, rearing on its hind limbs, struck Thrax viciously across the face. Bright blood filled the space between them and Thrax slipped, lost his footing and floundered, before surging upward again.

In that brief instant of separation, one true arrow sliced through the air and found its mark, straight through the creature's skull. Aleksia, with steady arm and steadier eye, had taken her shot and killed the beast.

"No!" Thrax couldn't help but howl as the creature stiffened and then slipped silently down into the river. It was his!

His eyes flashed green and Kira, watching from the bank, felt a sudden chill as the face of her rescuer changed from the elf she knew into something quite different, something hideous and frightening. It was only for a moment, and then the elves were rushing forward to help their hero from the water.

It seems odd now that Thrax didn't think to question how a creature so large and dangerous had managed to crawl into the channels of Heath Downs. Perhaps he could claim distraction, as unlikely as that would sound. It did in fact occur to him later, but he never had the opportunity to share the information with the Goblin Lord; by that time his mission had changed.

CHAPTER 32

*T*here was, of course, much rejoicing. Thrax was thanked more than he thought necessary for saving the life of one silly elf. Still, he was becoming ingratiated to the community and that, even he recognized, could be invaluable to his cause.

Both he and Kira were bundled in blankets and hurried to The House where Thrax received medical care. Though he tried to wave the surgeons away, his cuts were stitched and his wounded hands were salved and wrapped. As the bandaging was completed, Finn burst into the dispensary. His eyes were shining with his mother's light.

"A horse!" said Finn, smiling, and he looked suddenly younger and less like the soldier. "My gift to you will be one of our horses. You will choose any one that you like."

"No!" said Thrax, trying not to show his alarm. "It is too much!"

The wolf had seen through the charm cast by the talisman. What if the horses did as well?

"Too much for saving my life and now my sister? Not nearly enough, I would say," Finn exclaimed warmly as he clapped Thrax on the back. Happily Thrax had become somewhat accustomed to this type of contact and refrained from striking the elf.

Finn couldn't imagine anyone turning down the gift of one of the Strong family's horses. He thought that Thrax, being a noble and righteous elf, did not expect to be rewarded for taking action that was not heroic in his own mind, but only a matter of course.

"Because you are brave and selfless, you think everyone is," Finn continued, "but few elves would have had the courage to go into the water and fewer still would have survived if they had. Do not let your great humility stand in the way of your accepting my gift. Come. Choose your horse, and then we will all celebrate together."

Now Thrax feared that if he protested further he would only raise suspicion, so he smiled, shook Finn's hand and thanked him most profusely and properly. You can be sure that as they headed toward the stables, his mind was solely and actively engaged in pursuit of a plausible explanation in the event the horses would not come near him.

On approaching the first paddock, Thrax immediately found his concern was justified. The horses that had moments before been grazing quietly, raised their heads, eyes wide, with nostrils flared testing the wind. Finn whistled, but the horses would not come to the fence. Instead they pranced and shied, tossing their silky manes and pawing the earth with their steely hooves.

"Something has spooked them," said Finn. "Let's go though the barn and see the ones that have been brought up."

A certain number of horses were routinely housed in the barn with access to small exercise areas so that they would be readily available if need arose. These were rotated on a daily basis so that none were confined for long. Finn walked on and Thrax reluctantly followed.

"Ah," Finn exclaimed, "now here is a nice one."

He reached to stroke the neck of the charger standing in the first exercise yard. It lowered its head to him, then saw Thrax and reared back, snorting in alarm. The rest of the horses followed suit, all running to the furthest corners of their pens.

"I don't understand," Finn said. He looked around, and then fixed his gaze on Thrax, a question in his blue eyes.

"Maybe all the goblins I've killed have left their scent on me," said Thrax hopefully.

His explanation sounded weak in his own ears. Finn frowned, his eyes wary, but then suddenly he relaxed and laughed.

"The beast! Of course! How thoughtless I was to bring you out here without letting you clean up first. You must smell like the beast."

You think I stink? A faint memory stirred, causing Thrax to hesitate.

Then he saw the colt. It had been drinking water from its trough when Thrax had come out of the barn, but raised its head when the first horse sounded the alarm. Now it stood still, watching, not prancing or snorting, just watching with its bright emerald eyes. After a moment, without looking to left or right, the colt walked straight toward him.

"Does this one not know?" Thrax asked himself, moving cautiously forward.

The colt stopped at its gate and lowered its beautiful head as Thrax approached. Thrax reached to pat its sleek neck, looking in wonder at the cold green eyes. The colt didn't flinch, but Thrax could sense a drawing away as he stroked it. In that instant, though he couldn't say why, Thrax was certain the colt knew exactly what he was. Why then didn't it run?

"Excellent! Excellent! You could not make a better choice. This is an outstanding animal!" Finn enthused. "He was the last foal of my sister's favorite mare. She calls him Storm because he was born the night of a full force gale."

Thrax considered as he stood with his hand on Storm's shoulder. There had been a horse. It was so long ago. What was her name?

"Rosie," Thrax said, almost to himself, and an odd smile came to his face.

"That's right," Finn looked surprised, and then pleased. "Did Kira tell you about Rosie?"

"Yes," Thrax lied, nodding his head. He silently resolved to ensure Kira talked about the old mare the next time they spoke. That should be easy enough since he could tell her about the colt. It would seem natural to bring up his lineage.

"So your horse has chosen you!" Finn was overjoyed. "Should I call the groom? Would you like to take him for a short run?"

For just a second Thrax saw the eager little boy he had once known. A fleeting sense of something like sadness hovered near his heart, but then the coldness quickly returned.

"I would like nothing better," he lied again. "Unfortunately, my hands are rather torn up and I'm afraid I can't give him much of a ride. Perhaps tomorrow."

He extended his palm to show how the blood had soaked through the bandages.

"But I can't tell you how grateful I am for the honor of owning one of your family's horses. I am most undeserving." And he bowed as he spoke.

Relieved as he was over this unexpectedly fortunate turn of events, Thrax couldn't shake the feeling that the colt's glittering eyes were following him as he and Finn walked away and headed back to The House.

CHAPTER 33

*H*e found her sitting alone, outside in the dark. It had started to rain, and she was under the gazebo to the right of the tiled walk. The merry crowd in the main hall had made Thrax almost ill with their toasts and their praise. He had to get away from the revelers before he lost his patience and killed one of them, and so he slipped out into the garden. He never imagined that he would find Kira there.

The lamps in the hall, shining through the windows, created shadows among the trees and reflected in the puddles on the tile. Thrax froze, hoping Kira had not noticed him, but too late. She reached out a hand to him and he moved reluctantly to her side.

"What are you doing out here alone, my Lady?" Thrax asked politely, bowing and kissing her hand.

He couldn't help feeling slightly smug. He had become very good at pretending to be an elf.

"I'm not sure," Kira answered hesitantly. "I felt as if I couldn't breathe in there."

"Are you unwell?" he asked and at the same time thought how ridiculous he sounded. "Unwell" indeed.

"I don't think so," Kira sighed. "I'm feeling quite lost."

Thrax was silent. After a moment, she continued.

"Don't mistake me, I am very grateful for what you did for me today, but at the time I almost wished you had not been there to save me. I almost wished I had died."

At that she sobbed and buried her face in her hands.

"Damn and damn," thought Thrax in amazement, "she did want to die."

He couldn't think of anything to say. Thrax was enraged.

"What's wrong with her? Why did I risk myself to save her? She's pitifully weak!"

He stepped closer and put his hand on her shoulder as he had seen Finn do. In this case, it was a false gesture of comfort. He could barely restrain himself from snapping her neck.

Kira reached up and squeezed his fingers with her small hand.

"I know it sounds incredibly selfish of me. I have so much to be thankful for, but I miss my parents so. I guess I never fully recovered from their deaths."

She cried softly as if she would never stop.

"Can you possibly understand?"

"No," Thrax said slowly, truthfully, "I can't understand. I never knew my parents at all."

"I'm so sorry," said Kira, looking up at him in the dark, "I didn't know."

"My parents died shortly after I was born. I never knew them to miss them. I did lose someone later, though," Thrax continued, trying to make up a good story as he went, "someone who was like a parent to me."

It was best, he had learned, to make his lies close to the truth. He found that made them easier to remember.

Prompted by an alien impetus, Thrax sat down next to Kira and took her hand.

"I was young, only ten years old or so, and a very kind family took me in. The woman of the house was…well, she was kind."

"Kind" seemed grossly adequate, but Thrax could think of nothing better.

"She was the only person I had ever known, in my entire life, who treated me as if I mattered, as if I was important."

Thrax fumbled for words to describe feelings he had never expressed and Kira listened in silence.

"I'd never met anyone else like her. She was…I don't know exactly what she was. I would have done anything for her. I would have died for her."

His voice fell and Thrax suddenly realized that he was struggling to describe his feelings for Clare.

"When she died, I was with her, but I could not prevent her death. I watched as her life faded from her eyes and vanished. I felt a great hole, a vast emptiness open up in the

Wide World that could never, ever be filled."

He found he could not look at Kira. She was no longer crying, but was staring at Thrax in wonder.

"I am not an educated elf," he said, firmly, "but I know this. Your parents would not be proud of you for letting their deaths shadow your life. Continuing to grieve for them does not honor them in any way."

Kira reached up and wiped something that could have been rain from Thrax's face. She let her hand rest softly against his cheek.

"You have a great heart," she whispered. "I thank you sincerely for saving my life. I will no longer shame my parent's memory or diminish your heroism by giving in to such detestable self-pity. Amias and Clare Strong did not raise me to be such a coward."

They both stood up, and Thrax couldn't help but think that Kira seemed taller somehow. She took his hand in hers as they started back toward the house. At that moment there was a clatter of boots running over the stones toward them.

"Kira! I've been looking everywhere for you."

A young elf rushed up and swept Kira into his arms. He kissed her hard on the mouth, and then spun her around. Kira laughed with delight.

"What are you doing here? When did you get back?"

She seemed to have forgotten Thrax, who stood awkwardly to one side of the twirling couple.

The elf finally set Kira down.

"I heard about what happened! I left immediately from Cross Corners to see for myself if you were alright."

"I'm fine," Kira exclaimed, "and here is the warrior who saved me!"

Now she beamed at Thrax and reached for his hand again. Before he could stop himself, he pulled away. Kira's eyes showed a momentary surprise, nevertheless, she continued the introduction.

"Devin," she said, "this is Jac Savitch. Jac, this is Devin Thornehart."

"The younger son of the King," Thrax thought, "I should have known from the way Finn teased her about him."

Prince Devin was regularly stationed at Cross Corners due to increased skirmishes with the goblins at the western border. Thrax had known of him, but had given him little thought.

Though he felt an instant and intense hatred of the young elf, Thrax behaved as the situation demanded. He did bow rather low, but that was to be expected when being introduced to a prince. It showed respect, and had the added benefit of hiding any murderous intent Thrax might have harbored from showing in his eyes.

"Let's all go back to the party," said Devin. "I haven't

even seen my father yet."

"Please excuse me," Thrax replied, "but it is getting late and I am working with Finn on strategies in the morning. I hope to see you both again, perhaps tomorrow."

This was not offered with as much deference for the prince or his Lady as might be considered appropriate, but as Thrax was the hero of the day, fatigue was allowed as an excuse. Devin and Kira were too happy in their reunion to notice this small lapse in manners.

"See you tomorrow then," Kira called back, laughing as she and Devin ran through the rain. They were soon lost in the glare of lamplight.

Thrax turned and headed toward the barracks, a dark and solitary figure, his expression as black as the night. The wind was high, but as he passed through the garden with his head lowered against the drizzle, Thrax heard a faint rustling in the hedge. He stopped and his eyes glowed green. The wolf. He smiled grimly.

The next morning, Kira was surprised to find the wolf absent from his usual place at the foot of her bed. Nor did he turn up later in the day or ever again. Though she missed him, Kira consoled herself with the belief that he must have finally decided to return to the wild.

"Perhaps he's found a mate" she thought, "and will have pups of his own."

You and I of course know better. Kira's wolf, regrettably, met no such happy end.

CHAPTER 34

*T*hough the gift of a horse had seemed a near catastrophe the day before, Thrax woke the following morning to the realization that a horse might be his key to the city, in a manner of speaking. What could be more natural to an elf than taking his favorite steed out for an afternoon gallop? If only the steed would cooperate.

Determined to learn if Storm would in fact submit to being ridden by a goblin, Thrax crept from his bed in the early light of dawn and hurried down to the stables. Ducking through paddock fences to avoid alarming the horses in their stalls, Thrax approached the colt's exercise yard. He was surprised, and perhaps a bit unnerved, when he discovered Storm standing at the corner of the corral as if waiting for him.

Lifting a halter from a peg at the gate, he strode boldly across the enclosure, hand out for the colt to smell as he had seen the elves do. Thrax hadn't bothered to notice that the elves usually had an apple or carrot for their horses in their outstretched palms. The colt stood where it was; it did not snort or prance, but its emerald eyes glittered in the pale morning light.

Thrax patted the colt's nose and then its neck as he pulled the halter over its beautifully shaped head. Storm was perfectly quiet, so Thrax grabbed a handful of the colt's white mane and vaulted almost gracefully onto its back. There was an explosion of sorts; earth and heaven turned over twice, and Thrax found himself lying on his own back, breathless as he stared at the faint crescent moon.

He looked to see the colt pitching wildly around the corral, snorting and squealing each time its stiff legs hit the ground. Thrax sat up, shook his head and frowned. This was the second time he had landed in the dirt in the past two weeks. Slowly he climbed to his feet.

Storm completed one more circuit and then, as suddenly as he had started bucking, he stopped. The colt stood still as stone. His cold green eyes glinted and his nostrils flared blood red.

Thrax had never been one to recognize or admire beauty in the conventional sense, but something about the colt, its defiance of him, its fierceness and control, filled him with admiration.

"Beautiful!" Thrax said aloud, both stunned and disturbed by the experience of an emotion so alien. "Beautiful!"

Storm tossed his head and then walked deliberately across the paddock to Thrax. Thrax did not reach to pet him. Storm was not a pet. They simple stood together quietly as the sun climbed above the trees, chasing the faded moon from the sky.

CHAPTER 35

*T*he captain of the guard is teaching me strategy," Thrax chuckled coldly as Josef scratched symbols on a piece of paper.

"It's amusing to me that the elves taught me how to kill and now they are teaching me how to wage war."

"You enjoy killing," Josef remarked, without looking up.

He and Thrax had been meeting regularly for the past month. Josef had lost much of his superior attitude once he recognized that despite Thrax's obvious incorrigibility, he was remarkably intelligent. He was also singularly suited for his mission and was providing invaluable information to the detriment of the elves. The strain of duplicity that anyone else must have felt had no effect whatsoever on Thrax. He was comfortable with betrayal.

"Yes," growled Thrax harshly, "I do enjoy killing. I miss it. I miss the way it feels. I miss the way it smells. I miss the way it tastes."

Struggling to maintain the appearance of decorum, Josef nevertheless shivered inwardly; the response no doubt Thrax intended to produce. Thrax found it freeing to speak with Josef in this way, the only living soul he could speak to this way. He sometimes wondered when he would kill Josef and if he might even miss Josef once he was dead.

"You must enjoy it as well," Thrax added after a moment.

"Because I am involved in a war?" Josef asked. He shook his head. "That does not mean I enjoy killing. You should remember that the ultimate goal of war is peace."

"Through the complete and total destruction of your enemies!" Thrax laughed without humor, but his comment apparently disturbed Josef.

"I am not like you," Josef insisted, a bit defensively.

"You're right," Thrax smirked. "I enjoy and relish the murder of One-one troll, one goblin, one man, even an occasionally Werebeast," he paused. "Well, okay, anything that can put up a fight. But even I don't tread on Pixies. You want to destroy a whole race."

Josef did not reply, and so Thrax continued.

"And why the elves, of all people? They are the least offensive, most like sheep of any of the races. They're helpful!" he sneered, infusing the word "helpful" with unbridled contempt. "It's unbelievable that your Goblin Lord hasn't accidentally killed them all by now."

Josef's golden face flushed an unusual shade of amber.

"You do not know of what you are speaking," he stammered, his characteristic composure visibly shaken. "The elves started this war!"

Thrax opened his mouth, and then closed it again. Despite himself, he started to laugh, really laugh. Josef's eyes flashed with anger, but he held his tongue as his face flushed deeper orange.

"You think the elves started the war?" Thrax choked.

Josef could see that he had lost what little respect Thrax might have held for him. He felt a twinge of fear.

"These elves? You are the one who does not know of what you're speaking!" Thrax mimicked Josef and then snorted in disgust.

His report finished, Thrax turned to go, but the talk of murder had aroused his appetite. Instead of heading west through the woods and back to Heath Downs, Thrax left Storm tethered near the clearing and set out at a lope toward Castalia Spring.

Slipping the talisman into his pocket, he trotted steadily northeast along the river until Loch L'Aurin was within sight. He couldn't risk killing too near Heath Downs, at least not at present. In any case, Thrax had often found a watering hole to be a satisfactory site for stalking prey.

CHAPTER 36

*D*isturbed by the assessment of, to Josef, a heinous, bloodthirsty murderer, the golden goblin hurried quickly to his temporary home. He had a campsite just south of Loch L'Aurin, hidden among the dense trees of the Wuthering Wood. It was a convenient location for hunting, though he did not hunt for himself.

"I'm here," he whispered, as he stepped into the circle of light provided by the small campfire.

A figure hunched over the fire, turning a spit that held what appeared to be the remains of a new fawn. Josef grimaced involuntarily at the carcass, but then forced a smile as dark green eyes met his amber ones.

"I saves it for you." The speaker seemed somewhat surprised at her own words.

"Thank you," said Josef, kindly, as he reached to stroke her hair.

"Water is new, in the barrel besides the shade."

Josef smiled again at her attempt at gentile discourse. She was really trying and he loved her for her efforts, though he wasn't naïve enough to be convinced she felt the same. It was very likely she did not.

The figure stood and moved awkwardly to put her arms around him, an expression of affection he had taught her. She was a small goblin, not golden by any means, but an ordinary goblin, well, ordinary except that she happened to be Josef's wife.

"I'm nothing like Thrax," Josef assured himself as he embraced Grette. Someone like Thrax couldn't feel love, couldn't care for another as he did.

You'll remember that I told you goblins didn't have friends or families to speak of, and this had long been true for all the nomadic goblin tribes throughout the Wide World. Their individual survival precluded the establishment of close relationships. It was unheard of for a goblin to marry.

"Damn and damn," Thrax thought as he peered from the shadows of the trees. It seemed to him as if nothing had surprised him in fifteen years and now he was astounded by something new every day.

CHAPTER 37

*T*hrax awoke early the following morning, but lay in his bed staring at the low ceiling of his cottage. While the sky turned from midnight blue to the red-orange of dawn, he remained, quietly fingering the fetish at his neck. His taste of the open air the night before had awakened his wanderlust; how he had longed to stay in the Wuthering Wood, under the stars, free of the elves and the stifling environs of Heath Downs. Yet, he had returned.

Espionage. It had sounded so very interesting, but was all too much talk.

"Not for me," he decided.

Sighing heavily, he crawled from his covers, wondering what mischief the new day might bring.

CHAPTER 38

While Thrax reassessed his career options, Josef set out to relay his report to Lord Maelstrom. Though he had been keeping his master informed by messenger, this was to be his first personal appearance since he had departed the goblin fortress seeking Thrax.

He traveled along the west side of the Carrick Mountains, through the pass at Cross Corners and then skirted Mount Mourne until within sight of the Lowland Fens. It was a ten-days' journey on foot, but the weather was fine and he met with no hardships along the way. He was greeted with great enthusiasm; his information was obviously eagerly anticipated, and he submitted his full report concisely but completely.

Unfortunately for Thrax, and ultimately for Josef as well, Maelstrom was not pleased to hear of Thrax's opinion regarding the war. The fact that Josef had the impudence and imprudence to repeat it to him was an affront to the Goblin Lord and was felt as almost representing an act of treason.

As it happened, Maelstrom was also a golden goblin. He and Josef had apparently once shared a close personal relationship, making the younger goblin feel comfortable confiding the details of Thrax's sociopolitical commentary to his Lord. Though Maelstrom concealed his displeasure from his young disciple, he subsequently initiated actions that, had they been known to Josef, would have appalled him.

Happily for Josef, he was allowed to continue believing his master's propaganda for a short while longer.

Lord Maelstrom had hoped to enslave the Elven race intact. He now determined that he could only conquer the elves by eliminating their rulers and therefore decided to assassinate King Thornehart and all of his heirs. Ideally he would have delegated this task to Thrax as he had tentatively planned when recruiting him; however, Thrax no longer appeared to qualify as a reliable resource. Luckily for Maelstrom, he had many other resources at his disposal.

CHAPTER 39

*I*n spite of his decision to end his foray into the field of Espionage, Thrax stayed on at Heath Downs throughout Josef's absence. Although he rode out on Storm almost every day and told himself he longed for freedom and his former life, he returned each evening to the elves. Well, not exactly to the elves. Truth be told, though he was far from domesticated; no one, of course, has ever domesticated a goblin; Thrax had become quite lazy. Not that he would have admitted it, but a dry bed and rations served at regular intervals do provide a much less worrisome style of existence than stalking one's prey in the wild.

Without the wolf to shadow his steps, Thrax roamed widely within the city and, as he became more comfortable in his surroundings, began to revert to his natural and nocturnal habits. As a result, on the eve of Josef's fateful meeting with Lord Maelstrom, Thrax made a discovery of some import.

The bell in the watchtower was still vibrating, having struck the last toll of midnight, as Thrax crept along the inner wall, north of the gate. He noticed immediately that the sentries were on alert and was preparing to retrace his steps, when he saw a familiar figure hurrying across The Quarter. It was Prince Nolan, aroused from his bed, his dark hair ruffled, his arm in a sling. He wore a white nightshirt under his cloak, the tail tucked unevenly into his pants, bespeaking the haste in which he had dressed. Thrax drew back into the shadow of the wall and waited.

To say that visitors at midnight were unexpected and unwelcome at Heath Downs in those days of constant warfare would be to understate the elves feelings, nevertheless, there were certainly visitors at the gate. It took a great deal of conversation to convince the sentries to allow them to enter the barbican, and even more before the portcullis was raised.

They were three in number, all dressed in white. As one of them turned, Thrax saw his face clearly in the moonlight.

"Men!" whispered Thrax in amazement.

CHAPTER 40

*H*is speech had been well received; his constituents, such as they were, seemed pleased with his plans. Lord Maelstrom congratulated himself as he left the podium, basking in the adulation of his devoted followers. Josef, who had spent the night in the goblin fortress to rest before his journey north, followed him down the long corridor and into his study.

"My Lord," Josef began slowly, closing the door behind him, "I understand that conquering the elves and commandeering their technology and assets will vastly improve the lives of our people."

"Obviously." Maelstrom was feeling expansive, intoxicated. He could still hear the crowd shouting his name.

"But, we have been battling the elves for fifteen years. Thousands of goblins have died in that time. Might it not be better for everyone to negotiate a truce with the elves?"

"What?" Maelstrom looked at Josef as if he were speaking Troll. Josef plunged boldly onward, afraid that if he stopped now he would never dare broach the subject again.

"We could propose a treaty, a trade agreement that would benefit both our races. Would not that be a worthy solution? Would that not be the more appropriate action of an enlightened, civilized..."

"You are saying that I am not enlightened? You are saying that I am not civilized? You are saying we should admit defeat, stop the war, humble ourselves before the elves who have attacked us, bow down to them as superior to us and beg for crumbs?" Maelstrom's face flushed and his eyes bored into Josef's.

"Of course not, My Lord!" Josef was horrified at the reaction he had invoked. "I meant nothing of the kind!"

"You are saying that I did not understand you?"

"No! Yes!! I mean..."

"What then are you proposing?" Maelstrom hissed between clenched teeth.

"I...I am proposing nothing, My Lord," stammered Josef. "Please forgive me. I, of course, lack your experience and insight into such matters as war. Forgive me."

Maelstrom studied his lieutenant for a long moment, something of an idea taking shape in his mind.

"Because of our shared heritage," he began finally, "and because you were almost like a son to me, I will forgive you. But, do not impose upon me further or ever speak to me with such familiarity in the future."

"No," Josef gasped, relief flooding his face, "No, of course not. By your leave..." He turned to go, but Maelstrom raised his hand, halting Josef's hurried passage from the room.

"One moment," the Goblin Lord sniffed regally.

"On a different topic, how would you assess Thrax's commitment to our cause?" Lord Maelstrom asked, and Josef wondered at this sudden turn in the conversation. He hesitated.

"I don't know that I would describe Thrax as committed, My Lord," he said carefully.

"How loyal is he then, to you, to us?" Maelstrom faced the window with his back to the room. He seemed to be studying something far in the distance.

"To be frank, Sire, I am not sure that Thrax is even loyal to Thrax. He seems to go the way the wind blows on any given day."

"Then it may be time to terminate our association with him." Maelstrom glanced briefly over his shoulder at Josef, and then turned back to the window. "You will see to it."

Josef frowned. "You want me to tell Thrax we no longer require his services?"

"I want you to terminate Thrax."

Now Josef, as you know, had a high opinion of his own talents and worth; however, he had no delusions of immortality. True, he had never actually witnessed Thrax in combat, but based on the results of the contrived attack upon Prince Nolan he felt convinced that, even with a garrison of goblin soldiers, he could not prevail against him.

"My Lord, a physical confrontation with Thrax could only be expected to end in my death." Josef minced no words. Lord Maelstrom obviously did not appreciate the risk he was asking Josef to take.

"Thrax trusts you. He would not expect you, of all goblins, to attack him." Maelstrom continued to stare into the distance. "It should be easy..."

"Thrax does not trust me!" Josef exclaimed in spite of himself, "Thrax does not trust..."

"Do not interrupt!" Maelstrom's voice rose sharply. "Do as I say! I do not want to see you again until you bring me his head!"

And then, Josef knew. The goblin he had called "uncle" when a lonely child, his teacher and mentor and now his master, was sending him to his death. He stood for a moment, studying Maelstrom's profile, hoping to see a change in his countenance, hoping for a sign of reconciliation or regret. But, no sign came, and Josef walked slowly and sadly from the room.

CHAPTER 41

Now Josef correctly surmised that for him to make an attempt on Thrax's life would only result in his own death. His lord and master obviously wished him to die. Josef's only reasonable course of action was to take Grette and escape from the immediate area, to lose himself somewhere in the Wide World. But, where to go?

His distinctive features would make it impossible for him to stay hidden anywhere in the East. He shivered as another possibility crossed his mind. If he ran, would Maelstrom let him go? Or, would he send someone to hunt him down? Would he send Thrax?

Whatever he decided to do, it was imperative that he think clearly, that he plan carefully. Josef took a deep breath. He needed help, or at least he needed insurance against known threats. He needed an ally, and there was only one goblin he knew that might be able to preserve his life long enough for him to evade Maelstrom's sphere of influence.

But, where to go? Where to go? There was only one place he could think of where Maelstrom might not dare follow. Home. He could go home, if only he remembered the way.

CHAPTER 42

*T*he two great goblins that arrived in Cross Corners claiming to be emissaries of the Goblin Lord were met with suspicion by the elves. Their request to arrange a peace caucus was viewed as most assuredly a deception. Still, under heavy guard the goblins were escorted to Heath Downs and received by the King.

To the surprise of all, a gathering of Lord Maelstrom and his advisors and King Thornehart and his counselors was proposed to discuss the terms of a treaty. The elves believed it to be a trap. When he learned of it, Thrax, as Jac, could not resist pointing out to Finn that it was certainly a trap. Desperation can be a strong motivator, however, clouding judgment and driving otherwise sane creatures to insane acts.

The King wanted peace for his people. He wanted to stop their dying. And so, he agreed to an early date, a place and a time. When the fateful day arrived, his congress, his younger son, Devin, Finn, and three squadrons of the elves' best warriors attended King Thornehart. Kira accompanied her brother, inspired by the historic nature of the conference, but also to take advantage of the rare opportunity to spend time with her betrothed.

Though Thrax expressed an interest in the caucus, Finn requested he remain behind to provide security for the city and to watch over Prince Nolan who was not fully recovered from his brush with death earlier in the spring.

The meeting took place at Cross Corners, and, to the surprise of all, proceeded with apparent success. The King and his counsel met with a goblin they believed to be Maelstrom for three days and nights. On the morning of the fourth day the assembly adjourned; though much progress was made, there were areas of contention that the King felt he must discuss with his people.

All was pleasantries and promises to rejoin soon as the parties prepared to go their separate ways, and then an arrow sliced through the early morning air and struck the goblin leader in his chest. He fell, dead.

"The elves have betrayed us!" roared the goblins.

"No!" cried the elves.

"Kill them all! Leave none standing!"

And the battle raged. As you know, Cross Corners was a border town, and then a military outpost designed to withstand attack from goblins outside the boundaries of the pass. But now, the invaders were within the gates. The goblins howled and ripped into the closest elves driving them further into the settlement as the few civilian elves and their children scattered.

Cross Corners forces, led by Prince Devin, rallied and threw the goblins back, as the Heath Downs' guard rushed to protect their king. Though he was a fair strategist, Erron Thornehart was not, nor had he ever been, a warrior king.

As his soldiers fought to contain the goblins, his personal guard, led by Finn, sought to quickly remove him to safety, the object being to return him to Heath Downs in an acceptable state of health.

Heath Downs was less than two day's ride, but the horses that had been saddled in anticipation of the journey home were still waiting in the stables behind the barracks. As the elves fled on foot east and north through the compound, goblin soldiers, anticipating the elves' route, moved to intercept them.

"Archers up," Finn called, and half of the guard turned to face the pursuing goblins, some shielding their bodies behind trees while others dropped to one knee in the grass.

"Fire at will!"

A barrage of arrows rained upon the goblins, but many were deflected by their armor. The goblins fired back and pikes spiraled through the air.

Kira, not officially part of the guard and not wanting to lose sight of her brother, had been running with Finn, but turned to see Aleksia fall, impaled through the heart. Finn and the guard were beyond the compound, hurrying the king through the trees, trying to reach a defensible position in the foothills. Without a thought for her own safety, Kira turned and, picking up Aleksia's bow, began firing volley upon volley into the pursuing horde.

Goblin after goblin fell before her, but the raiders appeared to have inexhaustible numbers. Finally out of arrows, Kira threw her bow at the nearest and scrambled to flee, but too late. The goblins were upon her! She felt them ripping at her clothes and hair as she fell to the ground.

Kira fought, scratching and clawing for her life, and then everything dissolved in pain and darkness.

CHAPTER 43

*B*ack in Heath Downs, Thrax strode through the city, caged. He had spent days conversing with and ease dropping upon elves in a futile attempt to learn more about the men who had arrived in the middle of the night. No one spoke of them or seemed to know anything about them.

Thrax had no doubt that the meeting with Lord Maelstrom at Cross Corners was intended to entrap the elves in some way, but did the men have any role in it? The timing of their arrival suggested that they might.

Though during his sojourn in the Southland he had hunted men in their own ecosystem, he knew only of them as prey. Through practical experience he had learned that, of his most common victims, elves were the most difficult to catch, goblins, the hardest to kill, and men, well, men sadly were the most likely to provide entertainment.

Generally easy to catch and limited in their defensive skills, men hardly met Thrax's standards for prey. It's likely he would not have hunted them at all had he not found their reactions so very amusing. They were invariably shocked by his appearance and he had been told once, during one of his rare visits to a tavern, that few men believed in the existence of goblins and even fewer believed in elves. Which made it all the more interesting that these particular men knew about Heath Downs and had arrived in the middle of the night.

Driven by an uncharacteristic curiosity, Thrax sought out Prince Nolan. Nolan expressed optimism regarding the caucus, optimism it is unlikely he felt, but his formality of manner discouraged Thrax from broaching the subject of men and so Thrax left, strangely dissatisfied.

The human visitors, the talks of peace, should have been nothing to Thrax. Even while acting as a spy, he had had no investment in the outcome of the war. Still he felt a vague uneasiness and overwhelming restlessness. He expected the trap at Cross Corners had by now been sprung and only waited impatiently for word as to the form the betrayal had taken. His expectation, as you know, proved true and he did not have long to wait.

CHAPTER 44

*F*inn did not see Kira fall; he was too intent on protecting the King. But after a forced march through the mountains and once Erron Thornehart was safely within his keep, Finn's most urgent need was to locate his sister.

Word of the goblin attack preceded them and both Prince Nolan and Thrax, in his guise as Jac, met the surviving guard, counsel and the King at the gate. Finn left the officials to explain what had happened while he immediate set out to gather his troops. Thrax followed him across the grounds.

Finn was the first to speak.

"It was all a trick," he said, though unnecessarily. "I must take reinforcements to Cross Corners and I must find Kira."

Thrax nodded. Though empathy was an emotion he could never experience, Thrax nevertheless recognized the reasonableness of Finn's fear.

"I will go with you."

"No," said Finn. He paused and looked at Thrax with a curious expression on his face. Thrax couldn't quite make it out. "I would prefer you stay and guard the King."

I believe for a moment Thrax actually felt disappointed. After all, he was a warrior of some renown, a hero among the elves, besides being the most successful killer alive. Finn should have welcomed his help and interest. He opened his mouth to argue his point, but then thought better of it.

"Of course I'll protect your king," he said.

CHAPTER 45

*F*inn and his troops left within the hour and Thrax wandered out to the stables. He had begun to question why Josef hadn't mentioned the attempt to be made at Cross Corners. He also wondered if Josef knew anything at all about the men.

His instincts told him something important had changed in the goblins' approach to their war. Thrax decided it might be prudent to have a discussion with Josef, and so he saddled Storm and rode out. It was not the appointed time for a meeting, but Thrax, of course, knew where Josef and his wife camped near Loch L'Aurin.

A hint of panic showed in Josef's eyes when he recognized his unexpected and obviously unwanted visitor. Thrax, who was accustomed to invoking that type of response, thought little of it. As I mentioned, he planned to kill Josef at some future time so was not surprised that Josef was beginning to resemble prey.

"Why didn't you tell me the goblins were planning to kill the elves' king?" Thrax never used the term "we" when discussing goblins, no more did he do so when discussing elves.

Now when Josef had initially learned of the caucus, he had clung to the hope that Lord Maelstrom had a change of heart following his proposal for peace. He wished fervently to believe that dissident elves had fired the arrow that had killed the goblin leader and initiated new hostility between the fractions. The proof of the lie was that the goblin presenting himself as the Goblin Lord at the conference was not Maelstrom.

Maelstrom had sent Kayne, a close advisor and one of his guards, to impersonate him to the elves. Though Kayne was not golden, he had worked with Maelstrom long enough to present an apt imitation of his mannerisms. In spite of rampant rumors regarding Maelstrom's appearance, no living elf had in fact seen him. Josef was certain that Kayne had not been killed by elves, but had been murdered by one of Maelstrom's soldiers as an excuse for assassinating the elves' king. Josef paused as he considered how much, if any, of his speculation he should share with Thrax.

"I did not tell you because I did not know."

Josef chose honesty as the response least likely to inspire contempt. He had no intention of attempting to carry out Maelstrom's order regarding the disposal of Thrax, but had not yet determined how to request his help. He knew he couldn't appeal to Thrax's better nature or sense of right. Thrax had neither, as far as Josef could tell.

"But you don't deny it was a trap?" Thrax growled softly as his eyes narrowed. He had not expected the truth so freely revealed.

"I believe it might have been."

"I understood that Maelstrom wanted to enslave the elves, not wipe them out."

"Plans may have changed." Josef was purposefully vague. Thrax looked at him sharply.

"And my services?"

"Are still required as far as I know."

"And would you tell me if they were not?"

Josef hesitated for a fraction of second, but too long.

"No," he said, "I don't believe I would."

Thrax laughed his cynical laugh.

"I'll see you soon," he promised, and Josef felt a chill to his bones.

CHAPTER 46

*T*he conversation with Josef had intrigued Thrax; he felt he needed to learn more about Maelstrom's altered strategy and most importantly if and how he might benefit from this change in plans. Though he had lost interest in Espionage, there might be other opportunities available for someone with his talents. And so he tracked Finn and his soldiers where they had ridden southwest along Castalia Spring toward Mirror Lake and then Cross Corners. It was fortunate for Finn that he did.

The reinforcements that Finn had led to the outpost had successfully suppressed much of the violence in the town itself, but pockets of goblin soldiers still battled along the borderlands. On not finding Kira with Devin, Finn had taken those few soldiers Devin could spare and had started out to search for his sister.

Some hours later, Finn discovered a scrap of cloth similar to that of Kira's riding cloak on the edge of the grasslands between Cross Corners and Mount Mourne. A few moments later he and his elves came upon a squadron of goblins. Seconds later, before Finn and his soldiers could creep away, the goblins discovered the elves.

The elves had no chance; they were too few, and so they fought and they died. By the time Thrax arrived, less than ten elves were standing and all were seriously, if not mortally, wounded.

When Thrax had rescued Nolan and his guards from the goblins in the Wuthering Wood, it had been under orders from Maelstrom as part of a ruse to infiltrate the Elven community at Heath Downs. In choosing to join the current conflict, Thrax might just as easily have taken off the talisman and fought alongside the goblins. He didn't. It may have been that the elves were too weak to be suitable prey. It may have been that there were just more goblins to kill.

Leaving Storm hidden in a stand of brush, and dismounting on the run, Thrax howled savagely as he drew his sword. I agree it would have been wiser of him to approach the goblins with stealth and some amount of caution, but that was not his way.

With reckless abandon and something akin to joy, he threw himself into the fray, wielding his sword with such agility and skill that he might really have been an elf. Only three of the defenders were standing, but for Thrax this scarcely mattered. His was not a rescue mission; he only wanted to kill, and the goblins died and died. Some fought well and some fled in fear, but few escaped.

The violence of it was frightening, even to me: blood and bone, severed limbs, howling, yowling, roaring and sobbing; the elves said Thrax killed hundreds that day. The goblins, of course, denied it, claiming Thrax killed only a few and those being deserters and scavengers who lacked the skill to fight. I, as a witness, can assure you that the elves exaggerated little.

Suddenly there was silence and Thrax turned slowly around. None were standing: no goblins or elves. The ground was slippery with blood and sweat, and Thrax moved carefully through the fallen as if wondering what he might have lost. It was then that he heard someone calling his name.

CHAPTER 47

"*T*hrax."

Finn struggled to rise, but fell again, landing amongst the torn bodies in the dark, stained grass. Thrax hurried to him, but then stood confused as he realized Finn had called him "Thrax" and not "Jac". He touched his neck; the talisman still hung from its chain.

Unable to determine how best to respond, Thrax was silent as he assisted Finn to his feet. Moving cautiously, he helped the elf hobble over and stand beside a lone, stunted cottonwood tree, it's white, skeletal limbs stretched desolately toward the sky. There were no other signs of life.

"How long have you known?" Thrax asked finally, as he removed the chain from his neck and slipped the talisman into his pocket. There was no gain now in denial.

Finn studied his companion's hideous visage. I can't help but believe he must have been appalled. As with the young of all creatures, even goblins have some measure of softness, of appeal in their youth that fades precipitately with adulthood. Finn had not seen Thrax since Thrax was eleven. Needless to say, he had changed. Still, Finn spoke calmly.

"I knew from the beginning that you weren't what you seemed. Though we were grateful for your help, I think all were somewhat suspicious of you, an elf arising from nowhere, claiming to be from the West."

"But you let me stay, so you obviously didn't think I was a spy."

"We let you stay, but we controlled your access to information. You only saw and heard what we chose to share."

Thrax chuckled. "Is that so?"

In retrospect, everything had gone a bit too well. Perhaps he had underestimated the elves. Thrax did not feel this a failing on his part. Instead he found it mildly amusing.

Finn gripped the tree for support. His face was pale and his left leg dangled from the threads of ligaments and tendons that held his shattered knee together.

"But, I knew exactly who you were when you saved Kira from the creature in the river."

"Because of the horses?" Thrax was curious. What had given him away?

"No." Finn's face was tight with pain and he could barely speak through clinched teeth. "I knew it was you because I know you."

Thrax stared at Finn, his jaw slack, as shock and wonder struggled for dominance in the expression on his face.

"You know me? You know me?" Thrax was incredulous. "Then why didn't you turn me in? You of all people know what I'm capable of, what I've always been capable of."

"I never believed half of what I heard about you. No one else knows you, but I do. Because you pulled me from the river. Because you saved me and brought me home again. Because, in spite of our differences, in spite of everything, we were friends."

"You were a child. We were both children. That was before…"

"Look, I know what my grandfather and everyone else thought, but even then I never believed for one minute that you killed my mother."

"But I did," said Thrax. His green eyes were empty, his hollow voice, bitter.

"What?"

"I killed her."

The last bit of color drained from Finn's face and his knuckles turned white as he gripped his grandfather's sword.

And then, Thrax did perhaps the strangest and certainly one of the most noble things I had ever seen him do. He dropped down on one knee before Finn. He bowed his head.

"I killed her."

"No!" Finn's handsome features contorted in anger and agony. "No!"

"I killed her."

"But you loved her! I know you loved her!" Finn's voice was desperate, pleading. He was almost sobbing. "You're lying! You couldn't have done it!" He raised his sword threateningly.

"I cannot love as you do, but I cared for your mother, perhaps more than my life," Thrax said softly, and, I felt, from his heart. "I would have fought for her. I would have killed for her and died for her, but I could not have saved her."

"Then why?"

Thrax seemed strangely self-possessed; knowing that the time for truth had finally come. I suspect it was a relief for him to tell Finn, whatever the consequences might be.

"There were too many of them. She couldn't run because of the baby. I was young. My right arm was still weak. I couldn't carry her from the house. If I had fought, I would have died, leaving her alone with the goblins."

Thrax paused, searching for words even a goblin found hard to say.

"She asked me to… I thought she wanted me to… We saw them kill your father, but her death would not have been so quick. She knew what they would do to her, and to the child. She needed me to help her, to protect her… from that, from them."

Dusk was falling. The woods were suspended in silence

as Thrax waited quietly, as I think, for the fatal blow.

Anguish and understanding shown in Finn's eyes as tears streamed down his tortured face.

"I thought I knew you," he choked.

The stern soldier melted away and Finn was five years old again. His thin frame shook with the force of his sobs. The sword fell useless from his hand. Thrax looked up.

"We have to find Kira," Finn cried softly.

"I will find her."

Finn nodded. He knew Thrax would.

"Will you take me home?" He spoke in a whisper, a child afraid of the dark.

"I swear I will," promised Thrax.

Thrax stood and picked up Finn's sword. Holding it in his left hand, he supported his friend with his right as they moved slowly away from the killing field. For a moment, as I watched them carefully picking their way through the broken, lifeless bodies, I was touched with sorrow for all they had lost, but then memory buoyed me and I smiled. I remembered a cool, spring day long ago when a goblin had jumped from a bridge to save an elf. As the light faded around me, washing the colors from the palette of the day, I could almost have sworn I saw a tiny elf and a hulking young goblin laughing as they raced together through the Bluefield Marsh.

CHAPTER 48

*K*ira awoke to pain she had not known, the wonder being that she woke at all. A coarse bag, smelling strongly of decay, covered her bruised head and face, hiding from her sight the dankness of her tiny cell. Her battered arms were bound tightly behind her back, the leather thongs cutting into her flesh. It required all she had to raise her head from the floor. She was not alone.

All around she could hear the skittering sounds of many tiny feet, but none of their owners touched or approached her. There were enough of those no longer living in this prison to satisfy their needs.

Kira had been badly beaten, almost to her death, but that was all, and she thanked the Great Creator for his mercy.

Waves of agony washed over her, dragging her down and she wished for the release of unconsciousness again. She had no idea where she was, having been carried for what seemed like days by a variety of goblin soldiers. No food or drink had passed her lips during that time, or since.

"Help me," Kira cried weakly, but no one answered or heard. "Someone please help me."

She thought of Devin, envisioning his face, his soft, brown eyes and tender smile: her poet prince who wrote her sonnets, her friend and companion since a child; Devin, who hated the war almost as passionately as he loved her; Devin, who cried for every life he took and every soldier he lost; Devin, so different from his brother, Nolan, to whom duty and responsibility were all things.

The pain and stench overwhelmed her, driving Devin from her mind. Moaning softly, she slumped forward, laying her cheek against the ground. Even through the bag, she could feel the cool, solid earth and something else: a vibration perhaps. Somewhere far distant she heard the sound of steadily dripping water.

Fragmented thoughts whirled through her brain as she sought to make sense of a senseless world. Where was she? Goblins had caught her; by all rights she should be dead. Why then was she still alive?

Another face replaced Devin's in her mind's eye: the image of Jac Savitch, sitting in the palace garden in the rain, talking of loss and honor. The memory of Jac's face evoked a different response that at first intensified her despair, but then slowly the hope to live, the wish to live faded and was replaced with an iron determination.

"I am alive because I still have a part to play. With the Great Creator's help, I will not die here in this place."

She felt suddenly as if her mother were near and struggled to grasp the strength of faith she had held as a child. Fear ripped hope from her fingers, but she refused to surrender the shreds. Kira drew a deep breath. Though it hurt her body, it settled her mind.

"Someone may come for me," she thought grimly, "but I cannot wait. I must find a way to escape."

CHAPTER 49

*I*t took the better part of four days for Thrax and Finn to complete the journey home to Heath Downs. Finn was terribly hurt and could hardly help crying out as Storm carried him carefully through the scrub and grass and finally through the woods below the escarpment while Thrax walked at his side. Thrax had wanted to stop at Cross Corners to obtain medical assistance for his friend, but Finn, eager to waste no time in initiating the search for Kira, had obstinately refused.

Finn had not shared his suspicions of Thrax's true identity with anyone, not even his Prince; he could not have been believed in so outlandish a supposition. On his return, he was compelled to convince Prince Nolan not only that Jac Savitch was his boyhood companion, but also that Thrax, despite his reputation as a ruthless killer, could be relied upon.

The Prince did not share Finn's high opinion of the goblin, but held his peace; the faith he lacked in Thrax, he had in Finn. They decided to keep the secret among them; Thrax would not be safe within the city if others knew.

Prince Nolan was visibly shaken by the loss of Kira and wished to accompany Thrax in his quest. Thrax, who had no intention of acceding with this request, was noncommittal; there was no cause to argue at present. He needed more information regarding Kira's possible whereabouts before he could determine the best course of action.

He thought it unlikely that Kira was alive. Goblins have never been known for taking prisoners, a characteristic that had created a great deal of frustration for Lord Maelstrom from the very beginning. Thrax was later to learn that Maelstrom had not meant for all of the Surreydale elves to die that day so long ago. Some in particular he had hoped to capture.

While Finn rested in the infirmary, Thrax returned to his room near the guardhouse to change his clothing and wash up. He found it incredible that Finn had known who he was all along. How could Finn possibly have recognized him?

Thrax stood and gazed at his reflection in the mirror over his small dressing table. He was not a handsome elf as Finn was, nor even attractive like Nolan or Devin. Still, he looked a respectable elf. There was certainly nothing goblin-like about his reflection.

Carefully he removed the talisman and laid it on the table. His hands changed before his eyes and he looked up to see a now unfamiliar face staring back at him.

Goblins rarely give thought to appearance, though obviously the more frightening they look the more successful they are likely to be within the constraints of their chosen lifestyles. In that respect, Thrax was far and away superior to his peers. He nodded, satisfied.

He was what he had always been. The talisman had changed him only in the superficial, not the essentials, and perhaps the essentials were want Finn had somehow seen.

Well, his days of passing as an elf were over. It was time for Thrax to embrace his inner goblin to the fullest. It was time to find Kira, if she lived, but first he would find Josef.

CHAPTER 50

"Y ou are embarking on a mission to rescue an elf?"

Josef could not have been more astonished if Thrax had expressed a wish to become a celebrant.

"Yes," Thrax answered, without pause. "As I said."

It would not have occurred to him to clarify his cause to Josef; he cared nothing for Josef's opinion.

"Where does Maelstrom hold his prisoners, if he manages to capture any?"

This expression of derision, and the leer that accompanied it, reassured Josef that he was, in truth, speaking with Thrax, savage, sadistic, implacable Thrax. Still he could not resist asking the obvious question.

"Why?"

Now those of you who have been following this tale from the beginning may believe you have the answer to Josef's query. Perhaps, you might propose, Thrax's regard for Clare and confession to Finn had brought about a miraculous alteration in his character, transforming him from a bloodthirsty murderer into a righteous, selfless champion. If so, I regret you are to be disappointed.

"It will amuse me." He shrugged. And, sadly, it was so.

Josef stared. "But you are a goblin. The goblins are at

war with the elves."

Clearly, attempting to reason with a goblin is unwarranted and, in all instances, unwise. Thrax gazed coldly at Josef.

"I am a goblin. Maelstrom is at war with the elves."

"Sedition!" exclaimed Josef, before he could stop himself, forgetting momentarily that he, himself, was seeking a way to escape Maelstrom's sphere of influence.

Thrax's eyes glowed green. Quicker than thought, he had Josef by the throat, lifting him from the earth and effectively stifling any further unsolicited commentary. Josef's eyes bulged as he sputtered for breath. On the edge of his graying vision he could see Grette, who had faded into the woods on Thrax's arrival, crouching behind a tree, but she made no move in his defense.

"I doubt she will," sneered Thrax, as if reading Josef's mind, "but if she does, she's dead. She may be dead in either case. Now tell me what I need to know."

Josef nodded his assent, but Thrax continued to hold him suspended, relaxing his grip slightly to allow the passage of speech.

"Yes," Josef choked, his voice a hiss. "Yes". He gasped, "If the elf is alive, she will be held at the Tinsbury Dam, on the southwestern face of Mount Mourne."

Thrax abruptly released his hold and Josef fell to the ground. He did not attempt to rise, but sat there in the dirt, his eyes lowered in shame and his face bright orange with humiliation. He who had thought himself so noble, so far and above his fellow goblins; how easily the words had spilled from his lips; how quickly he had betrayed his Lord.

"Don't be afraid," Thrax said, though his voice was incapable of soothing. "Should I make it in and out again, I might reconsider my opinion of you. I might even feel that I owe you a favor."

"A favor?"

Josef clambered awkwardly to his feet, dusting his pants, as he sought to determine if Thrax was in earnest or perhaps baiting him. He desperately needed Thrax's help, now more than before, but Josef's self-conceit made it almost impossible for him to ask, especially to ask someone who aroused his disapprobation like Thrax did. His glance confirmed that Grette was still just outside the clearing. She hadn't deserted him.

"I..." Josef swallowed, "I..." He stammered as his face glowed umber. "As a matter of fact, I would like to request your assistance in a matter of some importance."

A flicker of something like surprise crossed Thrax face, but he recovered quickly and then sniffed imperially as Josef was wont to do.

"That being the case," Thrax replied regally, "I will certainly seek you out upon my return."

CHAPTER 51

*I*n a different time, when men ranged freely throughout the Wide World, the Tinsbury Dam had been built to harness the power of Loch L'Orren and the Durbin River, to provide light, heat and other comforts for their homes. Long since abandoned by the men who built it, the Dam was now being used by Lord Maelstrom to house dissidents and other prisoners who might prove of use to his plans. If Maelstrom learned that Josef had shared the location with Thrax for the purpose of insurgence, his retribution would be swift.

On returning to Heath Downs and arriving at the infirmary, Thrax was both perplexed and displeased to find both princes in attendance at Finn's bedside. Each had had the idea to lead a vanguard to scout for the goblins' stronghold and search for Kira. With great and uncharacteristic trepidation, Finn had convinced them to wait for Thrax's return.

At Finn's insistence, and against his own desire, Thrax was persuaded to share his intelligence regarding Kira's possible whereabouts, though he did not, of course, name his source. Nolan and Devin were each determined to participate in the imminent action. Thrax, recognizing that resistance was useless, unhappily acquiesced to accompanying a small company of elves in a reconnaissance operation. Due to his youth and superior level of fitness, Devin was chosen to lead the effort.

Of the four, only the younger prince seemed satisfied with the outcome and Thrax remained behind with Finn to voice his annoyance after Nolan and Devin had departed. As the door closed, Finn dropped his sanguine façade and lay back in his cot, pale and exhausted. Thrax had no mercy.

"Damn and damn!" he growled, his anger momentarily causing him to revert to his goblin roots. "Those stupid elves will be nothing but trouble. If I'm gonna do this, I don't need them bumbling around getting in my way!"

He seemed to have forgotten, and I believe often did forget, that Finn was an elf.

Finn tried a wan smile. "Perhaps you underestimate elves. You should give us more credit. After all, we've evaded Maelstrom for all these years."

"They'll get your sister killed," Thrax said, his voice rising. "Worse, they'll get me killed!"

Finn raised his hand.

"Please," he said, his sky blue eyes clouded with pain. "Please. Though they go with you, you are my hope. Please do not fail me, Thrax. Do not fail Kira."

The sheen of perspiration was rising on Finn's fair skin. Fever? Thrax paused in his tirade. Was Finn flattering him, playing to his pride to gain his cooperation? Thrax didn't believe so. He studied the young elf closely and then he spoke.

"You are a warrior of some renown," he said slowly. "If your sister lives, I will find her. If I find her, I will bring her home."

CHAPTER 52

*A*s you might expect, there were more volunteers among the elves than prudence would allow for a covert endeavor, affording Devin the opportunity to select those whose skills most closely matched his purpose. Of the chosen, all were weapons masters with experience in hand-to-hand combat and all were young save one.

Eight elves plus Thrax set out the following morning, so early that it was scarcely closer to dawn than the previous dusk. They dared not travel through goblin-occupied territory west of Mount Mourne, and so planned to traverse the grasslands and the Bluefield Marsh, hoping to gain access to the Dam from the Lowland Fens.

Their mission was formally classified as a reconnaissance, but Thrax suspected little information would be gathered and that it was most likely the elves would all die trying to retrieve Kira. It made no sense to him.

Of the eight elves in the company, Thrax recognized two, in addition to Devin. One was Liam, the tall, thin sergeant of the gatehouse guard. Liam had sparked Thrax's interest early on; unlike most elves, he was adept in the use of the short knife. In addition to those visible and immediately accessible, Thrax had discerned that Liam carried at least four blades concealed.

The other was the warrior Cathmor. Though grizzled and bent with age, the oft-decorated veteran had insisted on serving in the place of the injured Finn.

The rest were simply soldiers, individuals to whom Thrax had given no notice, but their names should not be lost nor their contributions forgotten. There were Keefe and Keegan, two brothers from Loaghaire. Keefe was most handsome, Keegan, fiery and determined. There was Dooley, the dark hero from Highborough upon Rione, and Druce, the courageous, a close friend to Liam. Gair was the youngest, and hailed from Cross Corners, his military service begun at the age of fourteen.

They set out together that fine summer morning. Their horses were fresh and their spirits were high. Cathmor took point, as was his custom. The rest of the company all fell in line. Storm bore Thrax boldly, and none suspected a goblin rode in their midst.

It was a journey of several days, through the grasslands and beyond. Though they faced trials in the Marsh and the Fens, the elves were skilled trackers and passed on without misadventure. It was not until they had almost reached the Tinsbury Dam that their plan went terribly wrong.

CHAPTER 53

*T*he metallic clank of the rusted bolt creaking within its casing startled Kira from sleep, but she felt only gratitude for the disturbance; it had not been a pleasant dream. Nightmare had transported her, pitilessly and inexorably, to the day of her parents' death. That ill-fated day had much haunted her as a child, but the memory had receded with time. Since her imprisonment, the specters of her dead parents were her most frequent and relentless companions.

Her jailer, a massive, hulking brute, entered and silently set a bowl of underdone meat and a flagon of mead on the rough bench that served as bed and table. Kira would have preferred water, clear, revitalizing, refreshing water, but accepted her portion without comment. She could not now remember how many days had passed before the goblins had deigned to feed her at all and she wasn't willing to risk withdrawal by complaining of the mead.

The meat neared rancid and the mead was unpleasantly warm, still Kira forced it down in hopes it might do her good. Her jailer stood by while she ate and then removed the bowl and flagon. She thanked him. With good fortune, the proceedings would be repeated in their entirety on the morrow. As to why her life had been spared, Kira could not guess.

The Leviathan, as Kira had dubbed him, was the only goblin she had seen since her capture and he was not communicative. When he had first come into her cell and removed her hood, she had shrunk from him in fear, but he had been strangely gentle while fixing a chain from her wrist to a ring in the wall. Yet, she had cried in terror and trembled at his touch, not realizing she hadn't been hurt until long after he had left her.

Days passed and Kira gradually became accustomed to the beast, even looked forward to his brief daily visit as the sole distraction from her ghosts. And so she greeted him, thanked him for waiting upon her, and tried to engage him in discourse with no success. He would not speak to her. In her heart, I think Kira was relieved. Soon she would be forced to make an attempt against his life, or, at the very least, an attempt to disable him. You see, there were no windows in her damp, vile prison and The Leviathan stood between Kira and the door.

CHAPTER 54

S ix days after Thrax and the elves departed Heath Downs for Mount Mourne, Maelstrom's messenger, Cronan, arrived unannounced in Josef's camp. Though his visit was anticipated, his orders, to escort Josef back to the goblin fortress, were not. Following Josef's last disastrous encounter with Lord Maelstrom, the golden goblin had thoroughly considered, but ultimately discarded, thoughts of flight. Instead he chose to maintain the appearance of normalcy until and if Thrax returned.

Not three weeks had passed since his last appearance before his master, thus Josef had no cause to expect a summons; clearly the Goblin Lord had grown impatient. Josef was naturally reluctant, and he expressed his hesitancy couched in the most politically astute terms.

"Are you refusing to accompany me?" Cronan inquired gruffly, not comprehending Josef's words, but deriving the import. "Will you defy the Goblin Lord?"

"No! Of course not!" Josef exclaimed hastily. "I simply need a few moments to prepare."

Glancing frantically about the camp, Josef privately despaired of finding any one item or any bit of information that would satisfy Lord Maelstrom in lieu of Thrax's head. Still, he would have to go. The messenger was a large goblin and armed. Josef, though remarkable learned and intellectually superior, was sadly lacking in any combat skills.

Fortunately for him, as he rummaged through his meager belongings, Grette completed her own assessment and decided to eliminate the threat. She was small, and neither educated nor particularly intelligent, yet she had lived long and successfully in the Wide World. When Cronan had arrived, Grette had grabbed the spit from the fire and faded into the woods. Sharp enough to skewer a wild pig, she surmised its tip would serve equally well on goblin.

Cronan did not seem aware of Grette as she crouched among the shadows. Seizing the opportunity when his back was turned, Grette sprang from the trees, shoving the spit through his back with force. Cronan toppled forward, as Grette vaulted into the air, bringing her full weight onto the grip and pinning him to the ground.

The stricken goblin's cries of agony filled the clearing, and Josef stood as if he were stone, his face benumbed in shock and horror. Grette had not intervened against Thrax. Why had she done so now? As Cronan writhed helplessly, impaled, Grette, unperturbed, moved quietly to Josef's side. Maelstrom's messenger did not die quickly, but he did die.

Josef had sometimes been appalled while watching Grette hunt prey and this was murder in the strictest, most brutal sense, committed without hesitation or apparent remorse. Though I suspect he was inwardly repulsed by her actions, nonetheless Josef took his wife's hand.

"We must go," he stammered slightly. "We must break camp."

She nodded, holding his gaze, forcing him to look into her eyes. To Josef's tremendous relief, he glimpsed no beast within, only calm, cool green. So they stood, silently, and then rousing themselves began gathering what supplies they could before moving off through the Wuthering Wood toward Heath Downs. There could be no returning to Mount Mourne. There could be no reliance on Thrax. Perhaps the elves would not kill him; with Maelstrom there could be no doubt.

CHAPTER 55

*T*he Lowland Fens lay south of Heath Downs and Surreydale, at the juncture where the majestic Rione spilled into Loch Donla. Covered with ice in winter and submerged by The Floods in spring and fall, the Fens were only passable in midsummer when the heat of the sun and receding water transformed them into hard, dry mud flats.

The skeletons of massive redwood trees littered the landscape, their roots immodestly exposed and often spanning twenty feet and more, creating a grotesque and eerie contour to the Fens. The giant trees had been swept from the Suraelian Mountains by the river and carried to their final rest thousands of leagues from their place of origin.

Direct forward movement was impeded by the debris, and the elves and Thrax made slow progress across the flats. Travel was by foot, the horses having been stabled with a farmer on the edge of the Marsh awaiting the company's return. Insects were plentiful and these, combined with the humidity, caused a gain of inches to seem miles. There was little talk.

The sun had reached her zenith and begun her descent, blindingly bright and hot, her heat shepherding the company toward the shade of the mountains. Devin had called a brief halt. While the others rested, Liam climbed higher to survey what lay ahead. When he climbed down again, his face was aghast; the dreamer's pale eyes startled awake.

Putting a finger to his lips, he motioned the others to follow him into a small recess between two tall chimneys of rock. It was there that he told them what he had seen.

Hordes of goblins, armed and in mail, were massed on the flats below the Tinsbury Dam. Poised to march, there could be no uncertainty of their purpose. Where the Goblin Lord had discovered so many goblins willing to embrace his cause was a mystery, but Maelstrom had obviously and at last abandoned his hope of enslaving the elves. He had decided to murder them all.

Acting quickly, Prince Devin dispatched Liam and Dooley to warn the elves in Cross Corners and Heath Downs. The remainder of the company would climb Mount Mourne, not entirely relinquishing their hope to find Kira, but shifting their focus to true reconnaissance on the eve of extermination.

CHAPTER 56

Lacking a window or any other source of light except that reflected from the dimly lit hallway through the narrow bars of her prison door, Kira had no means for delimiting day from night. Time, the intangible, lost meaning, being at once endless and fleeting, crawling at a snail's pace and then taking flight. The only point on which she could fix was the repeated and regular entrance of The Leviathan. The Leviathan appeared at consistent intervals, bringing her food and drink, but goblins being nocturnal, she suspected her once-daily meal might actually be arriving at midnight.

Five days previously, she had thought to begin placing a mark in the dirt for each visit by her jailer, but could not begin to orient herself to date. Her sleep was fitful and the chain at her wrist restricted her movements within her tiny cell. Though she was recovering from her beating, the wretched conditions and meager rations were sapping her strength. Kira knew if she hoped to escape her dungeon, she would have to act soon.

Not wishing to harm someone who had done no harm to her, Kira resisted the idea of killing The Leviathan. In actuality, it was unlikely that she could, but a distraction was needed that would prevent his pursuit when and if she managed to break her chain and flee. In this, her resources were scant. True, there was considerable refuse on the floor of her small living area, but nothing that could easily be adapted as a weapon; well, that is to say, except possibly for the bones of her dungeon's previous tenants. Of these, there had clearly been many and their scattered remains were plentiful.

CHAPTER 57

I have come to seek political asylum," Josef announced importantly, gazing with disdain at the Elven sentries that hailed him in the woods below the Carrick.

He and Grette had approached Heath Downs openly. Josef believed that the most advisable manner in which to approach one's enemies, being the least likely to be misconstrued.

Though the sentries wondered at his physiology, they were not impressed by his airs. Josef was mortified when, after being relieved of their possessions and undergoing an unceremonious search, he and his wife were marched up the ramp and into the city. The goblins were met by startled looks from the citizens, looks the goblins returned, neither, of course, having ever visited an Elven community before. Josef's expectations of primitive squalor were quickly overthrown.

The elves had no housing for prisoners-from-war, and so Josef and Grette were deposited in holding cells alongside the community's few and petty lawbreakers. You see, the goblins brought battles to the elves and those not killed on the field withdrew. The elves defended, but did not pursue. Josef, assessed as being no significant threat, was held with the general populace. Grette, possibly lethal and the only female in the detention center, was allowed a private room.

Word of the goblins' arrival was carried to the royal family; the King, out of bitterness for the deception at Cross Corners and hostility fed by fifteen years of war, declined to meet with them. Instead he sent Prince Nolan in his stead. King Thornehart, his health failing under the burden of constant care, had come to rely heavily on his son, trusting Nolan's judgment in all matters.

"I am a political refugee," Josef stated earnestly. "My proposal for a peaceful solution to the current conflict, a compromise, a sharing of ideas with your people, was not well received," An understatement, but essentially correct. "I and my wife have come to you, the elves, hoping for asylum."

Prince Nolan, though astounded by the application, maintained a respectful posture and expressed his willing-ness to hear Josef's plea.

Josef, taken aback by the King's perceived slight in not attending in person, and distressed to be relegated to someone he considered an underling was, at first, doubtful and reserved; as you'll recall, Nolan was not an imposing prince. As the dialogue proceeded, however, Josef could not deny that the Prince, while lacking the affectations of royalty, was in words and thoughts remarkably well mannered for a barbarian.

"Your appearance is very different from that of most goblins," Nolan remarked, an observation politely made that carried no affront.

"I am not from this place. I left my home as a child and traveled here on an expedition," Josef replied, and felt a flush of happiness from the memory. "My parents were explorers."

"How interesting and exciting that must have been," the Prince said.

Nolan's calm civility was drawing Josef out. Josef had had no one he perceived as near his equal with whom to converse for many years. He had not realized how alone he felt, how isolated he had become. Josef had been thinking of home so often of late, trying to remember. A thought occurred to him suddenly. The elves had, in different spans of time, inhabited much of the Wide World. Might they have knowledge of The Remnant? Should he ask? Josef hesitated. *This elf is my enemy and the enemy of my people.* The golden goblin set his jaw.

"I am here to discuss asylum," he said.

"And what is your vision of asylum?" asked Nolan. Josef's comments had piqued his interest and he would have liked to learn more, but wisely refrained from turning the interview into an interrogation.

"We will live quietly and peacefully among you, bringing diversity to your community through free and open communication of our cultural beliefs and mores," Josef offered magnanimously.

Prince Nolan considered.

"That would seem a very beneficent offer," he replied, standing and bowing before turning to the door. "I will certainly speak with my father regarding this opportunity."

Of course, Nolan recognized that Josef was being less than forthcoming with his information. He could only conjecture the reason for this unexpected petition for sanctuary. Still, the prince was willing to risk a great deal to end the war and housing two goblins in the community detention center did not seem to pose a significant threat.

For Josef's part, he naively hoped the elves could protect him from Maelstrom. He was not aware that the Goblin Lord had mobilized his army to lay siege to Heath Downs and raze to the ground all that was Elven in his path.

CHAPTER 58

W hile Josef sat uncomfortably in the corner of his cell, his arms crossed tightly over his chest, staring balefully at his curious cellmates, Thrax and the remaining six elves plotted strategy. Actually, the elves plotted strategy. Thrax had little to say in support.

Throughout the journey from Heath Downs, Thrax had struggled, resisting the urge to abandon the elves and continue his quest alone. And, in truth, Thrax was right. It would have been easy for him, a goblin, to enter the Tinsbury Dam and find Kira. He knew it was so, and yet, he had promised Finn; he had committed to the elves. Internal conflict was alien to Thrax, indecision, intolerable.

The elves had crept along the foot of the mountain as far as was consistent with safety. The goblins were camped all around them, and they could proceed no further on the ground. In order to gain an improved vantage point, the elves determined to climb Mount Mourne to a ledge approximately fifty feet above their current position. The mountainside was covered with sparse vegetation, but the sun was descending, casting most of their planned course in shadow.

As Thrax gazed at the near vertical ascent, a dark look clouded his face. I wonder now if he wasn't experiencing a premonition, a forewarning of the misfortune to come.

Keegan and Keefe took the lead, followed by Devin. Gair was assisting Cathmor, who climbed nimbly despite his age. Druce motioned for Thrax to precede him, and then started up in his wake. Progress was rapid. Four of the elves had reached the shelf. Cathmor was pulling himself over the edge. And then, Thrax fell.

Though he had the appearance of an elf, Thrax retained the clumsiness of a goblin. In spite of his efforts to climb quickly and quietly, it was Thrax who inadvertently led to the elves' discovery. Thrax fell.

A shower of pebbles rattled down the slope and thousands of goblins' heads turned as one.

"Damn and damn," Thrax muttered, frantically grappling for a hold on the mountain. "I don't want to die as an elf."

It would have been the end of Thrax then and there, for he could not have recovered himself, had it not been for the courage and alacrity of Druce. Spying the narrowest of ledges ten feet below and to the left, he launched himself from the cliff wall aiming for his plummeting companion. Hurtling through the air, the elf struck Thrax solidly from the side, his momentum carrying them both across the cliff face and miraculously to the safety of the rim. Landing with a thud, they scrambled to their feet and stared down at the seething mass of goblins below them.

"We've got to climb," Druce exclaimed breathlessly, smiling fiercely as he gripped Thrax's hand in solidarity. "We must reach the others."

Thrax nodded. The goblins were swarming up the mountainside, howling in rage, climbing over one another in their haste to rip the intruders to shreds. Druce started up with Thrax close behind. The elves on the shelf shouted encouragement and released a rapid volley of arrows to provide cover for their friends. Though they each managed to strike several of the closing goblins, five elves with bows obviously could make little impact on a juggernaut of thousands.

It was the warrior Cathmor, coolly surveying the landscape for a defensive point at which to make what must have been their final stand who came upon an idea for stalling Death, offering the elves the slimmest hope of escape. Sighting the edifice housing the Tinsbury Dam's controls, he gave a shout. The building was a short distance along the crest of the mountain, and it was unguarded. Believing themselves invulnerable in their own territory, the goblins, in their arrogance and conceit, had failed to post a guard.

"If we can release the water, we can at least delay the goblins' progress," he advised.

Devin ordered Keegan and Keefe to the dam while he and the others continued to fire over Thrax's head. It was a humbling experience; Thrax, killer of elves and disparager of their virtues, clinging to a cliff while Devin, Cathmor and Gair risked their lives for him. Thrax climbed as quickly as he could. Druce, lighter and more agile, had just reached the edge of the shelf when, in an instant, a pike launched from below struck him fair in the back and tore him from the cliff's face. Thrax looked up to see Druce fall. Druce did not cry out, as Thrax would have expected, but fell silently past him as Thrax ducked to avoid the scattering rocks.

The elves on the shelf went still, stunned, and Thrax's green eyes grew large. A roar went up from the goblins below, urging Thrax into motion again and he attacked the mountain like a living foe. At last he reached the shelf and Gair helped him over the rim. In consternation, Thrax stood for a moment, looking down, seeking Druce. The elf that died to save his life was nowhere to be seen. Thrax wanted to howl.

Scrambling to the top of the ridge, the elves and Thrax fairly flew across the mountain toward the dam. Inside the housing, the two brothers struggled frantically with the ancient mechanism that controlled the gates. A violent "CRACK!" sent a tremor through the earth, causing the elves to stumble and the goblins to wrestle for a hold on the craggy cliff. And then, the dam groaned, the floodgates opened, and water poured like tears down the face of Mount Mourne.

Thrax steadied himself and looked back, fascinated, as great sheets of water crashed into the nearest goblins, sweeping them from the rocks, plunging them down the mountain, and carrying them away. The goblins yowled in hatred and fear. Some kept their grip, but only for short seconds, before dropping sixty feet to the valley below. As the water flooded the plain, those troops on the ground were swept into the Durbin River and toward Loch Donla.

Watching the devastation of the goblin camp, Thrax found the experience singularly unsatisfactory. Though some of the goblins were killed, drowned in the crushing waves, most were dragging themselves sputtering and coughing from the water, virtually uninjured and eager to resume the fight. The company had bought time, but nothing more.

He sighed, wishing he had found a way to make the trip alone.

Keegan and Keefe rejoined the group, clapping each other on the back in a way that made Thrax itch to throw them both down the mountain. Druce was dead and goblins were on their trail.

"We must flee now, My Prince, to protect your life." Cathmor took the lead, scrambling along the ridge, heading north towards home. Thrax and the others followed, all except Devin. The young prince hesitated, looking at the dam. He had to have known the outcome, the utter hopelessness of his cause, before he made his choice. I have wondered since if he regretted it.

"I cannot leave her," he cried, turning from his companions and running toward the causeway.

CHAPTER 59

*L*iam and Dooley successfully crossed back through the Fens and the Bluefield Marsh, stopping occasionally for rest, but never to sleep. On reaching the grasslands and collecting their horses, they went their separate ways, Dooley riding hard for Cross Corners and Liam to Heath Downs.

The disruption caused by Thrax and his company had no significant effect on the mobilization of the goblin army. Though hundreds of goblins pursued them in the mountains, there were thousands upon thousands more moving through the Fens and toward the elves. Like a plague, the masses descended upon the Bluefield Marsh, cutting a swath through the land and leaving no living creature in their path. Innumerable goblins were lost in the bogs, but still the army marched on, burning the vegetation and feeding on the Marsh's denizens that fled before them.

The grasslands, dry from the summer heat, were tender to the flame. The fire erupted and spread almost instantaneously, devouring the plain. The Cross Corners forces made a stand and many brave elves died when the goblins crushed the resistance and burned the outpost to ash. Among them was Dooley, from Highborough on Rione, but his alert, arriving before the hordes, allowed many elves to escape through the mountains to the Carrick and Heath Downs.

CHAPTER 60

Something extraordinary was happening, she realized, and deep within the goblin stronghold at the Tinsbury Dam Kira crouched within her cell as the walls shook with peals of rolling thunder. Dust and plaster from the ceiling fell to the floor and Kira crawled under her bench for cover. It seemed her dungeon was coming down.

In rushed the Leviathan. Kira had never seen him in such a state. He did not notice her at first, and spun about the room before spying the direction of her chain and following it to her hiding place. Grabbing her by the arm, he pulled her out and both staggered as the earth moved beneath them.

Her heart was pounding as she waited, keeping her free hand behind her back. What would he do? Would he loose her from her chain? Or had he come to kill her?

As the giant goblin sprang for her throat, Kira, without hesitation, plunged her bone knife directly into his great green eye.

CHAPTER 61

*P*rince Devin raced across the causeway of the dam until he reached a ladder that descended into her depths. It seemed the Wide World was shaking, but in actuality the Tinsbury Dam, after centuries of restraining Loch L'Orren in his mountain home, was failing under the pressure of releasing her gates. The abrupt disturbance in the distribution of the lake wrenched apart the cracks and crevices and erosions of time, culminating in the dam's destruction.

Thrax and the others had no recourse but to follow the prince, though, had Thrax consulted only his own leanings, he would have left him. Keefe, Keegan and Gair, being younger and light, reached the ladder ahead of Thrax and Cathmor, and without pause hurried down. Thrax motioned Cathmor to precede him and stood undecided as the old soldier navigated the rungs.

He could still remove the talisman and slip down the mountain to enter the dam from below, find Kira, if alive, and take her to her brother. Descending into a goblin's den disguised as an elf, well, Thrax was not afraid of Death, but he did not choose it either.

The Dam moaned again, as great chunks of her stone skin shattered and fell. Shouts floated up to the causeway amid the sudden clamor of battle. Shaking his head, Thrax stepped down into darkness.

He found himself in a narrow passageway, so narrow in fact that the combatants could fight only two abreast. The elves were surrounded on both sides, four engaged in mortal combat while Gair lay dead upon the floor.

"Damn and damn!" This time he shouted his frustration. It was too close for swords, so Thrax drew his knife from his belt. He would have to be quick, and he was.

A strange sense of calm settled over the goblin, followed by mounting exhilaration, as he began to kill. This was what he had missed. This was what he knew. This was what he was meant for, his particular skill. The elves fought valiantly at his back as Thrax carved his way down into the bowels of the Tinsbury Dam, those that opposed him falling or fleeing in fear. It seemed none could stand against him.

And then the passageway turned, opening into a massive chamber where the goblin forces rallied, howling for vengeance.

Drawing their swords, the elves surged forward, and the battle raged.

CHAPTER 62

*I*t was a fearsome sight. In madness, the goblins flung themselves upon the elves, clawing and ripping at their flesh with no regard for their own harm. Grievously outnumbered, the elves were driven to the wall as Thrax's sword was stripped from his fist. Keefe fell bleeding from a strike to the head and Devin, stumbling over him, went down as well. Sure of their victory, the goblins rushed forward as Cathmor leapt to the aid of his Prince.

Wielding his sword, the famed warrior stood and absorbed the blow meant for the young elf. The blade of the poleax struck fair in his chest, splitting his breastbone and sending him to his knees. As his life's blood drained from the gaping wound, a profound peace settled upon his rugged face. No trace of fear shown in his steel-gray eyes.

Though Death claims us all, still many are astonished at its appearance when it comes for them. Cathmor had been in the company of Death so often that, though not truly advanced in years, he did not seem surprised at all when Death found him. Instead he greeted Death as an old acquaintance, if not a friend.

There was something so shocking about the great hero's passing that even the goblins paused in its wake. And then, Prince Devin rose to his feet and Thrax grasped a mace that lay upon the floor. Grief stricken and outraged, the elves fought back, as if nothing but blood could satisfy.

It was a feeling that Thrax knew well, and he recognized it and rejoiced in it.

Like demons they fought, or elves possessed, the two left standing and Thrax. Tiring of the mace, Thrax raised a halberd in each hand and spun out into the center of the floor. Devin joined him and fought at his back while Keegan guarded his fallen brother.

Wave upon wave of goblins fell and still they continued the fight. Until, there were none.

The earth quaked violently, sending showers of dust from the walls and ceiling that settled on the living and the dead. Keegan crouched protectively over his brother while Thrax reached to steady his companion. Devin looked at Thrax, flushed and smiling; but then his youthful face grew troubled as the Prince slowly sank to the ground. Thrax knelt at his side.

"You must find her," Prince Devin whispered softly, reaching to clasp Thrax's hand. Thrax searched urgently for the fatal wound, but there were many and too much blood.

As Devin looked into the face of his comrade-at-arms, his eyes grew suddenly wide. "What...?" he said, and then he died.

Thrax gazed at the prince for a moment, wondering what he had seen, and then gently he closed the young elf's eyes. And so, the warrior Cathmor died to save his Prince, but could not save him.

Thrax rose to his feet, threw his head back and howled. Grasping the chain, he ripped it from his neck, stalked across the room and pressed the talisman into Keegan's hand.

"Wait here with your brother," he growled, as Keegan shrank from him in alarm. "I will get the elf."

He turned and strode through the darkness into the depths of the Dam.

"This time they will know," Thrax promised himself grimly. "They will know exactly who's killing them."

CHAPTER 63

*H*e had meant to kill her all along, Kira realized as she dodged to evade his grasp. Tethered to the wall as she was, she could not escape her cell, but The Leviathan, with one hand over his ruined eye, could not quite seem to catch her.

The ground shook and The Leviathan lurched and still he refused to fall. Kira was tiring, her strength almost spent; nearing despair, she confessed the inevitability of her fate and asked the Creator his will.

From out of the ether, and the darkness that blinded her, Kira felt suddenly as if someone's hand had brushed her cheek, a warm, familiar touch.

"Devin?" she gasped as she turned, but no one was there, and that is when she knew. Her Prince was gone. He had left her forever alone in the Wide World. He had come to her to bid her goodbye. The Leviathan lunged and Kira could not move. She could not think. She could not breathe. She could not feel his hand as it closed about her neck.

And then, her prison door burst from its hinges and something far worse than The Leviathan stalked into the room.

CHAPTER 64

*P*rince Nolan stood alone on the battlements, watching the billowing black clouds of smoke that loomed to the south. They seemed closer, even closer than they had been an hour earlier when Liam arrived, haggard and pale, to warn of the impending goblin invasion.

Based on his estimation of the size of the army, and the forces needed to withstand it, runners had been sent to Loaghaire and beyond, advising all elves that their capital might soon be under siege. In fifteen years of war the elves had worked out a contingency plan for every conceived possibility but no plan had allowed for the massive numbers of invaders described.

"My people will die," thought Nolan, and he was afraid.

CHAPTER 65

*T*hrax was not sure of the way. All around him the dam was collapsing, writhing in her death throes as if a living thing. Kira, shielding her head with one arm as she clung to him with the other, stumbled along at his side. She had not known him, had not recognized him as her brother had done. But with all Kira had endured, the revelation that Jac Savitch was Thrax in disguise seemed as nothing.

Kira staggered, nearly fell, and Thrax lifted her in his arms. They had little time left. Thrax, having made short work of the Leviathan, felt it would be a pity to die now, under the rubble of the dam.

"Jac! Jac!" Someone was calling and Thrax began to run.

In the dust and darkness of endless passageways, the brothers from Loaghaire had found him.

Keefe had regained consciousness, and he and Keegan had waited as long as possible before venturing to follow Thrax. There had been a great risk that they might take a wrong turn and miss those they meant to find. But in this they were not cruelly used.

And so together, the surviving members of the company stumbled from the ruins, leaving more behind than they could bear. Had they known then what awaited them, their devastation would have been complete.

END OF BOOK 1